A Who's Who of the Viking Age

People, Legends, and Myths

Matthew Leigh Embleton

A Who's Who of the Viking Age

Cover: Miscellany on the Life of St. Edmund, 1130 - MS M.736 fol. 9v, Morgan Library

Acknowledgments

I have long been fascinated by history and languages, and my writing this book has been further inspired by the discovery that my DNA is 33% Scandinavian. I am very grateful to the special people in my life who have supported and encouraged me in my work. Thank you for believing in me. You know who you are.

Introduction

Who were the players? Where do they exist on the scale of history, legend, and myth? And how do we know? From the first raids by the mysterious 'Northmen' in the darkness of the 8th century, to the chieftains, earls, and kings who changed the development of Europe and influenced the medieval world, the Viking Age produced stories and accounts of unique figures in history preserved in oral tradition, and written in chronicles, and sagas.

With a distinctive culture, shaped by the bleak and unforgiving landscape of Northern Europe, the character and outlook of the Norse people was driven by the brutal reality of a struggle for land, resources, and survival. The varied geography of Scandinavia with its fjords, mountains, lakes, islands, and marshlands set the stage for developments in seafaring and boat building that were far ahead of the rest of Europe, allowing the bold and adventurous to travel further and further afield in search of routes for exploration, plunder, trade, and settlement.

Those who raided are today known as Vikings, a term coined in the 18th century at the beginning of a period of renewed interest in local mythology and folklore as a means of national identity (the Old Norse word 'víkingr' meant a sea-rover or a pirate). The sagas and stories of their activities were translated and later embellished to fit romantic ideals of the heroic warrior or the noble savage. Many of the popular misconceptions about the Vikings and the Viking Age come from this period.

This book outlines who they were, what we know about them from accounts at or near that time, and how each of these figures shaped the story of the age.

1.   The Beginning

Beaduheard: The First Victim

Beaduheard was born around the middle of the 8th century, and he was an Anglo-Saxon shire reeve ('shire reeve' or '*scir gerefa*' in Old English is where the modern English word 'sheriff' comes from).

Based in Dorchester, South West England during the reign of King Beorhtric of Wessex (786-802), he was the first known person to have been killed by Vikings in England.

According to the *Anglo Saxon Chronicle*, in the year 787 (789), three ships of Northmen arrived at Portland, near where Beaduheard happened to be that day, and he immediately rode out to meet them.

Not knowing who they were or why they had come, and perhaps believing them to be traders at first, he insisted that he take them to report to his king. As an important man of high rank, he would have been used to projecting a tone of authority when dealing with anyone who arrived in his jurisdiction, and he would have been used to compliance from those he spoke to.

These Northmen are believed to have come from Hardangerfjord outside Bergen in Norway, and it could well have taken them 3 to 6 days or even more to have reached this land, depending on weather conditions and the course they ended up taking. Relieved to have found land, but also cold, wet, and tired after a long journey they must have been in no mood to be barked orders at by anyone.

Who was this man that had come to meet them, they must have wondered. What did he want? Was he a threat? Was he suspicious of their activity? Had he found out or been tipped off somehow about their intentions, that they intended to look for suitable places to raid? Were they being arrested? Were they walking into a trap?

The tension, mistrust, and misunderstanding due to language differences must have rapidly escalated and finally exploded. The Northmen killed Beaduheard and his men on the spot. The *Anglo-Saxon Chronicle* entry for 789 reads:

"7 on his dagum coman ærest .iii. scipu Norðmanna,	"And in his days came first 3 ships of Northmen;
7 þa se gerefa þærto rad 7 hie wolde drifan to þæs cinges tune,	and then the reeve thereto rode and willed to drive them to the king's town,
þy he nyste hwæt hie wæron, 7 hine man ðær ofsloh.	knew he not what they were, and he the men there slew.
Þæt wæron þa ærestan scipu deniscra manna þe Angelcynnes land gesohtan".[1]	Those were the first ships of the Danish men the English kin's land sought".

---

[1] Anglo-Saxon Chronicle (B, The Abingdon Chronicle I), 787 (789): Cotton MS Tiberius A VI, ff 1r–35v 2021, 10th Century, London, British Library, 2012, f13r
<http://www.bl.uk/manuscripts/Viewer.aspx?ref=cotton_ms_tiberius_a_vi_f013r> Accessed 22/11/2021

Lindisfarne: The First Raid

When Vikings raided and sacked the monastery at Lindisfarne on the 8th June 793 it sent shockwaves throughout Christian Europe. The *Anglo-Saxon Chronicle* for 793 reads:

"Her pæron reðe forebecna cumene ofer norðhymbra land.
7 þæt folc earmlic bregdon þætpæron ormete þodenas 7 ligrescas.

7 fyrenne dracan wæron gesegene on þam lifte fleogende.
þam tacnum sona fyligde mycel hunger.
7 litel æfter þam þæs ilcan geares. on. vi. id. Ianr.

earmlice hæthenra manna hergunc adilegode godes cyrican in Lindisfarna ee. þurh hreaflac 7 mansliht.

7 Sicga forthferde. on. viii. kl. Martius".
[2]

"Here were dreadful forewarnings come over the land of Northumbria, and woefully terrified the people: these were amazing sheets of lightning and whirlwinds,

and fiery dragons were seen flying in the sky.
A great famine soon followed these signs,
and shortly after in the same year, on the sixth day before the ides of January,

the woeful inroads of heathen men destroyed God's church in Lindisfarne island by fierce robbery and man slaughter.

And Sicga died on the eighth day before the calends of March".

Alcuin of York: The First Commentator

Alcuin of York (c735-804) was an Anglo-Saxon scholar, poet, teacher, and clergyman from York in the Kingdom of Northumbria.

He was born around 735 and was a student of Archbishop Ecgbert at York before he was invited by Charlemagne (Carolus Magnus, Charles the Great) to be a scholar and a teacher at the Carolingian Court at Aachen in the Kingdom of Francia.

He remained active throughout the 780s and 790s, becoming one of the most important intellectual figures in a period of revival of study in literature, the arts, architecture, religion, and legal matters.

This would later be referred to as the Carolingian Renaissance, idealistically inspired by and seeking to emulate elements of the former Western Roman Empire, as a beacon of civilisation in dark and turbulent times.

News of the raid at Lindisfarne soon reached Alcuin, and he wrote letters to kings and bishops describing his horror at the unprecedented atrocity.

He also speculated on whether it had been some divine punishment for the sins of the Northumbrian people or the beginning of a much greater grief.

---

[2] Anglo-Saxon Chronicle (D, The Worcester Chronicle), 793: Cotton MS Tiberius B IV, ff. 3r- 86v 2021, 11th Century, London, British Library, 2012, f26v
<http://www.bl.uk/manuscripts/Viewer.aspx?ref=cotton_ms_tiberius_b_iv_f026v> Accessed 22/11/2021

Alcuin (middle), MS cod.652, fol. 2v, Vienna, Austrian National Library, 9th century

In a letter to Æthelred, King of Northumbria, Alcuin wrote:

"Ecce tre centis et quinquaginta ferme annis quod nos nric,
patres huius pulcherrime patrie incole fuim,
et nunqua talis terror prius apparuit in brettannia,
vel ut modo a pagana gente pessi sumus,
nec eius modi navigium fieri posse putabatur,
ecce ecclesia sancti cuthberti sacerdotum dei sanguine aspra,
omnibus spoliata ornamentis,
locus cunctis in bretannia venerabilior,
pagani gentibus datur ad depredandum".[3]

"Behold, it is nearly three hundred and fifty years since we in this kingdom,
and our fathers the most beautiful country have lived in,
and never such terror before has appeared in Britannia,
or by means of a pagan race suffered the worst,
nor in this way a navigation possible thought,
behold the church of St. Cuthbert priests of god blood spattered,
all stripped of ornaments,
a place of all in Britain more venerable,
the pagan race given to prey on".

---

[3] Alcuin of York, Letter from Alcuin to King Æthelred of Northumbria, c793, The Letter Book of Archbishop Wulfstan: Cotton MS Vespasian A XIV, ff 114–179 2021, 11th & 12th Centuries, London, British Library, 2012, f126r & f126v
<http://www.bl.uk/manuscripts/Viewer.aspx?ref=cotton_ms_vespasian_a_xiv_f126r> > Accessed 22/11/2021

2.   Ragnar Lothbrok: The Making of a Legend

Ragnar Lothbrok was a legendary hero, and a legendary king of Denmark and Sweden. He was born around 780 and died sometime after 865. His legend is made up of the accounts from around the time of his activities, the sagas that tell the story of his origins and deeds, and the poetry that was written about him. He is described in *Ragnars Saga Loðbrókar* as a large and handsome man:

> *"Hann var mikill vexti, vænn yfirlits ok vel viti borinn, stórlyndr við sína menn, en grimmr sínum óvinum".*[4]

> *"He was large grown, handsome to look at, well knowing and keen, generous with his men and fierce with his enemies".*

The sagas tell us that he inherited the throne of Denmark and Sweden from his father Sigurd Ring (*Sigurðr Hringr*). He was born Ragnar Sigurdsson (*Sigurðsson*), but his nickname Lothbrok (*Loðbrók*) translated as 'hairy breeches' or 'shaggy breeches' was given to him on account of the protective cow hide clothing he wore. *Ragnars Saga Loðbrókar* explains:

> *"Hann lætr gera sér föt með undarligum hætti, þat eru loðbrækr ok loðkápa, ok nú er ger eru, þá lætr hann þau vella í biki".*[5]

> *"He had made himself clothing in a strange way, they were shaggy breeches and a shaggy cape, and when they were made, he had them boiled in tar".*

A bronze plate depicting a warrior with shaggy breeches
Torslunda, Öland, Sweden, c6[th] to 8th century

Some believe that Ragnar Lothbrok was actually a combination of several different figures in history with similar names. Some of the accounts from around Ragnar's time were written in Latin, and so it was necessary to latinise the spelling of his name to give it a nominative '*-us*' ending.

---

[4] Embleton, M. L. (Translator), Ragnars Saga Loðbrókar (The Saga of Ragnar Lothbrok):, The Sagas of Ragnar Lothbrok: Norse Text, Translation, and Word List, 2nd Ed., 2021, London, Independent, 2021, p.14, ISBN 979-8475152591
[5] Embleton, M. L., 2021, p.14

Ragnar (*Ragnarr*) is a name of Proto-Germanic origin made up of '*ragina*' (counsel) and '*harjaz*' or '*hariz*' (army). It has many different variations and spellings.

Vandalic	*Raginari*
Old Norse	*Ragnarr*
Old English	*Rægenhere*
Frankish	*Ragenar, Ragnachar, Ragnahar*
Old High German	*Raginheri, Reginheri*
Latin	*Raganarius, Ragenarius, Raginerus, Ragnerus, Reginarius, Reginherus*
Danish	*Ragner*
Faroese	*Ragnar*
French	*Rainier*
German	*Rainer*
Icelandic	*Ragnar*
Italian	*Ranieri*
Latvian	*Renars*
Norwegian	*Ragnar*
Swedish	*Ragnar, Ragge*

It is tempting to believe that any sources mentioning any of the names above must refer to the same legendary Ragnar Lothbrok, however this is not necessarily the case. It is too much of a stretch chronologically for all of the Ragnars mentioned around that time to have been the same person. For example, there was a '*Ragenar*' who was a Frankish bishop of Amiens from 830 to 849, and a '*Reginar*' who was Duke of Lorraine in the Frankish Kingdom of Lotharingia sometime from 850 to 915.

Less common however is the nickname 'Lothbrok', of which there are also many variations in spelling: '*Lodbrok*', '*Lodebroch*', '*Lodparch*', '*Lodparchus*', '*Lothbrok*', '*Lothparch*', '*Lothparchus*', and '*Lothpardus*'.

The first mention of Ragnar appears in the *Annales Xantenses* as 'Reginherus'. It describes the Viking raids on Paris in 845. This was the culmination of a Viking invasion of West Francia, made up of 120 ships with approximately 4,000 men led by Ragnar. They received 7,000 pounds of silver and gold as payment for leaving. The account states that Reginherus died shortly after the raids, perhaps as divine punishment for plundering Christian sites. However, this may be merely Christian propaganda. Their fleet made it back to the Danish King Horik I, where it is also said that Ragnar soon died of a violent illness that also spread in Denmark.

"Postea vero ingenti clade percussi sunt predones, in qua et princeps sceleratorum, qui Christianos et loca sancta predaverat, nomine Reginheri Domino percutiente interiit".[6]	"But afterward the robbers were slain with a great slaughter, in which also the chief of the criminals, who had plundered Christians and holy places, by the name of Reginherus he perished when the Lord struck him".

---

[6] Pertz, Georg Heinrich (Ed.), Annales Xantenses (Annals of Xanten), 845: MGH SS rer. Germ. 12, 1888, Hannover & Leipzig, Die digitalen Monumenta Germaniae Historica (dMGH), 2004, p.14 <https://www.dmgh.de/mgh_ss_rer_germ_12/index.htm#page/14/mode/1up> Accessed 22/11/2021

This version of events however does not give time for Ragnar to have been captured and killed at the hands of the Northumbrian King Ælla. After which his sons raised the Great Heathen Army and invaded England in 865 to avenge their father's death, some twenty years later.

Ragnar is described as having had three wives:
- Thora 'Borgarhjört' Herraudsdottir (*Þóra 'Borgarhjǫrtr' Herrauðsdóttir*)
- Lagertha, (*Lathgertha, Ladgerda, Laðgerda, Hlathgerth, Hlaðgerðr*)
- Aslaug (*Auslag, Auslaug, Áslaug, Svanlaug*) also known as Kraka (*Kráka*) and later Randalin

Lagertha is mentioned in the *Gesta Danorum*, Aslaug is mentioned in *Krákumál*, *Ragnars Saga Loðbrókar*, and *Ragnarssona Þáttr*, and Thora is mentioned in all four of these sources.

Ragnar is also believed to have have had at least 14 children, some of whom became legends and historical figures in their own right. They are counted differently in each of the sources, including 2 unnamed daughters, and 12 sons:

- Agnarr
- Bjorn 'Ironside'
- Dunwat
- Erik 'Weatherhat'
- Fridleif
- Halfdan 'Hvitserk'
- Ivar 'the Boneless'
- Radbard
- Rognvald (Ragnvald)
- Sigurd (Siward) 'Snake-in-the-eye'
- Ubba
- Ulf

The *Gesta Danorum* and *Ragnars saga Loðbrókar* agree on seven of these sons. Halfdan and Hvitserk are variously mentioned but never together in any source, which has led to the belief among historians that they are the same person, i.e. Halfdan with the nickname of 'Hvitserk' (white-shirt). Only *Chronicon Roskildense* mentions 'Ulf' as one of Ragnar's sons.

According to William of Jumièges in his *Gesta Normannorum Ducum*, Ragnar ordered his son Bjorn 'Ironside' to leave his realm, as per the tradition of the times, and Bjorn went raiding in West Francia and the Mediterranean.[7]

Ragnars saga Loðbrókar and *Ragnarssona Þáttr* both tell the story of how Ragnar first won fame and the hand of Thora Borgarhjört in marriage.

He killed a giant snake guarding Thora's home. Originally the snake was very small in size, and it had been given to Thora by her father Herraud Jarl of Götaland. It was originally intended to be an amusement for her, but it had grown so large that it was out of control, and no one would go near it except to feed it an ox for each meal. Ragnar successfully killed the snake and avoided being poisoned by its venomous blood on account of his protective 'shaggy breeches'.

"Ok er hann kemr í skíðgarðinn, þar sem ormrinn var, leggr hann til hans með spjóti sínu, ok þá kippir hann at sér spjótinu.

"And he came to the fence, where the serpent was, and laid towards him with his spear, and then drew his spear.

---

[7] Guillaume de Jumiège, Gesta Normannorum Ducum (Deeds of the Dukes of Normandy), 1060: pub. pour la première fois en français par M. Guizot, et suivie de la Vie de Guillaume-le-conquérant, par Guillaume de Poitiers, 1826, Paris, Hathitrust Digital Library, 2019, p.11-13 <https://babel.hathitrust.org/cgi/pt?id=mdp.39015013753564&view=1up&seq=23&skin=2021> Accessed 22/11/2021

> *Ok annat sinn leggr hann.*
> *Þat lag kemr í hrygg orminum, ok nú vinst hann við hratt, svá at spjótit gekk af skaptinu, ok verðr svá mikill gnýr í hans fjörbrotum, at skemman skelfr öll.*
>
> *Ok nú snýr Ragnarr á brott.*
> *Þá kemr blóðbogi milli herða honum, ok þat sakar hann eigi, svá hlífa honum klæði þau, sem hann lét gera".* [8]

> He stabbed with his spear again.
> The spear shaft hit the serpent's spine, and he defeated it quickly, and the spear head came off from the shaft, and there was such a noise as the serpent died that the whole cabin shook.
>
> Now Ragnar turned away.
> Then a gush of blood struck him between his shoulders, but it did not harm him, because the clothing that he had made protected him".

Ragnar's marriage to Thora was sadly short-lived, and she died of a sickness. For a time, Ragnar was inconsolable. Sometime later Ragnar learned from his crew of a beautiful woman called Kráka (Aslaug). Soon after he met her and was impressed by her beauty and wisdom.

They married and had several sons, all of whom went on to achieve fame and success in their own right. Ragnar hoped to compete with the success of his sons by conquering England with only two large ships, going against his wife's advice.

Ragnar and Kráka (Aslaug), by August Malmström, c1880

Ultimately Ragnar was defeated and captured by King Ælla of Northumbria and was thrown into a snake pit to die.

---

[8] Embleton, M. L. (Translator), Ragnars Saga Loðbrókar (The Saga of Ragnar Lothbrok):, The Sagas of Ragnar Lothbrok: Norse Text, Translation, and Word List, 2nd Ed., 2021, London, Independent, 2021, p.15, ISBN 979-8475152591

"Varð hann um síðir handtekinn ok settr í einn ormgarð, ok vildu ormarnir ekki koma nær honum.
Ella konungr sá, at hann bitu eigi járn um daginn, er þeir börðust, ok nú vildu eigi ormarnir granda honum.

Þá lét hann fletta af honum klæði þat, er hann hafði yst haft um daginn, ok þegar hengu ormarnir á honum alla vega, ok lét hann þar líf sitt með miklum hraustleik". [9]

"He eventually became captured and set in a snake pit, and snakes would not come near him.
King Ælla saw that he had not been bitten by any iron that day when they battled, and now the snakes did not want to injure him.
Then he had him stripped of his clothes, which he had been wearing outermost during the day, and then the serpents hung upon him in every direction, and there he laid down his life with much bravery".

While in the snake pit, Ragnar imagined how his sons would react when they heard the news of his death, and muttered the immortal words:

"Gnyðja mundu grísir, ef galtar hag vissi" [10]

"How the piglets will grumble, when they hear what has happened to the boar"

The Death of Ragnar Lothbrok, by Hugo Hamilton, 1830

Krákumál was written from the point of view of Ragnar Lothbrok in King Ælla's snake pit facing certain death and reminiscing about a life of heroic deeds:

---

[9] Embleton, M. L. (Translator), Ragnarssona Þáttr (The Tale of Ragnar's Sons):, The Sagas of Ragnar Lothbrok: Norse Text, Translation, and Word List, 2nd Ed., 2021, London, Independent, 2021, p.100, ISBN 979-8475152591
[10] Embleton, M. L. (Translator), Ragnars Saga Loðbrókar (The Saga of Ragnar Lothbrok):, The Sagas of Ragnar Lothbrok: Norse Text, Translation, and Word List, 2nd Ed., 2021, London, Independent, 2021, p.70, ISBN 979-8475152591

"Fýsumk hins at hætta,	"Face this danger,
heim bjóða mér dísir,	Home invite me Disir,
sem frá Herjans höllu	Who from Herjan's hall,
hefr Óðinn mér sendar.	Has Odin sent for me,
Glaðr skalk öl með ásum	Gladly shall have ale with the gods,
í öndvegi drekka,	To drink foremost,
lífs eru liðnar stundr,	Life is passing time,
læjandi skalk deyja". [11]	Laughing I shall die".

The Great Heathen Army invaded England in around the year 865 led by Ragnar's sons. They wreaked revenge on King Ælla, defeating his army, capturing him, and killing him by 'blood eagle'.

The blood eagle is a legendary grim punishment consisting of carving an eagle into the victim's back, also described in more gory detail as opening up the back of the victim, severing the ribs from the spine, and then opening them out to resemble an eagle's wings.

The deeds of Ragnar Lothbrok and his sons live on in the sagas handed down from generation to generation. They were kept alive in oral tradition for centuries before finally being written down in the 13th century.

Lothbrocus and Sons Ivar and Ubba worshipping idols
Harley MS 2278 folio 39r, 15th century

---

[11] Embleton, M. L. (Translator), Krákumál (The Lay of Kraka):, The Sagas of Ragnar Lothbrok: Norse Text, Translation, and Word List, 2nd Ed., 2021, London, Independent, 2021, p.122, ISBN 979-8475152591

3.   Lagertha: The Shield-Maiden

Lagertha was a legendary Viking shield-maiden and ruler of Norway. Her story was told in the *Gesta Danorum* written by Danish historian Saxo Grammaticus.

Lagertha by Morris Meredith Williams, 1913

The name Lagertha is a latinisation of the Old Norse name *Hlaðgerðr*. The Old Norse letter 'eth' = 'ð' was latinised as 'd' or 'th', and the initial 'h' was dropped. Because of this, there have been many different spellings of her name (Hlaðgerðr, Hlathgerth, Ladgerda, Ladgerða, Laðgerda, Laðgerða, Ladgertha, Laðgertha, Lagertha, Lathgerda, Lathgerða, and Lathgertha).

Her career as a warrior began with a battle to defeat the forces of Swedish king Frø, who invaded Norway and killed the Norwegian king Siward (Sigurd). She distinguished herself on the battlefield and was key to Ragnar's success in defeating Frø:

"Inter quas affuit et Lathgertha, perita bellandi femina, quae virilem in virgine animum gerens, immisso humeris capillitio, prima inter promptissimos dimicabat.
Cuius incomparabilem operam admirantibus cunctis - quippe caesaries tergo involare conspecta feminam esse prodebat".[12]

"Among them was Ladgerda, a skilled amazon, who, though a maiden, had the courage of a man, and fought in front among the bravest with her hair loose over her shoulders.
Whose incomparable deeds were admired by all, for her locks flying down her back betrayed that she was a woman".

---

[12] Saxo Grammaticus, Gesta Danorum: Saxonis Grammatici Danorum Historiae Libri XVI, 1534, Switzerland, Universitätsbibliothek Basel, 2010, p.200 <https://www.e-rara.ch/bau_1/content/zoom/889580> Accessed 25/11/2021

Ragnar was impressed with Lagertha and courted her from afar seeking her hand in marriage. He visited her in the Gaula valley in western Norway, and was set upon by a bear and a great hound guarding her home. He killed the bear with a spear, and choked the great hound to death, thus winning her hand, as the story goes. Lagertha and Ragnar married and had three children, a son named Fridleif, and two daughters whose names are not known.

Ragnar later returned to Denmark where a civil war had broken out. In retrospect he was annoyed at Lagertha for having set the bear and the hound against him. He divorced her in order to marry Thora Borgarhjört (*Þóra Borgarhjǫrtr*), the daughter of King Herraud (*Herrauðr*) of Sweden.

Civil war broke out again in Denmark, and Ragnar sent to Norway for support, and Lagertha, who still loved him, came to his aid with 120 ships. During the battle, Ragnar's son Siward (Sigurd) was wounded, and Lagertha saved the day with a counter-attack:

"Lathgertha quoque, teneris membris incomparabilem sortita spiritum, trepidantis militiae studium specioso fortitudinis exemplo erexit. Militari namque discursu inopinatorum terga circumvolans, socialem metum in hostilia castra convertit".[13]

"And Lathgertha, in a tender frame, had acquired an incomparable spirit; She set up the pursuit of a perplexed army with a fair example of fortitude. Flying around the rear of the unexpected military maneuver, she turned allied fear into the camp of the enemy".

When Lagertha returned to Norway, she quarreled with her new husband, and killed him with a spearhead which she had concealed in her gown. She then took the whole of his name and sovereignty:

"Insolentissimus namque feminae spiritus absque viro regnum gerere quam fortunae eius communicare iucundius duxit".[14]

"For this most insolent spirited woman thought it pleasanter to rule without her husband than to share the throne with him".

Saxo momentarily breaks the neutrality of his commentary by describing Lagertha as "most insolent" for these actions, perhaps indicating a degree of misogyny which would have been commonplace among churchmen of the time. Since the adoption of Christianity in Denmark in the mid 11th century, ideas about the role of women in society changed dramatically, and for Saxo, these Viking shield-maidens were evidence of the chaos and disorder of the old heathen ways of Denmark, which he believed had been resolved by the Church and a stable monarchy.

Centuries later however, the legend of Lagertha has become the archetype of the shield-maiden, courageous, fiercely independent, and a Norse equivalent to the Amazons of Greek mythology.

---

[13] Saxo Grammaticus, Gesta Danorum: Saxonis Grammatici Danorum Historiae Libri XVI, 1534, Switzerland, Universitätsbibliothek Basel, 2010, p.202 <https://www.e-rara.ch/bau_1/content/zoom/889580> Accessed 25/11/2021
[14] Saxo Grammaticus, p. 202

4.   Aslaug: The Seeress

Aslaug (*Auslag, Auslaug, Áslaug, Suanlogha, Svanlaug,* also *Kráka,* and later *Randalin*) was a figure in Norse Mythology who appeared in the Prose Edda by Snorri Sturluson, the Völsunga Saga, and *Ragnars Saga Loðbrókar* as one of Ragnar's wives.

Kráka by Mårten Eskil Winge, 1862

She was the daughter of the Germanic heroic legends Sigurd (*Sigurðr*) and Brynhild (*Brynhildr*). After their death, Brynhild's foster father Heimir looked after Aslaug from the age of three. He became concerned that others would seek to murder Aslaug to destroy the family line. He made a harp large enough to hide her in, and then travelled the land as a poor harp player, carrying Aslaug in the harp along with his gold and silver wherever he went, stopping occasionally to bathe and feed her.

King Heimir and Aslaug by August Malmström, 1856

They arrived at Spangarheid at Lindesnes in southern Norway and managed to secure a place to stay with peasants Áke and Grima. They believed that Heimir's harp contained valuables, and Grima successfully persuaded Áke to murder Heimir in his sleep so they could keep the valuables for themselves. When they broke the harp open however, they found Aslaug who had not yet learned to speak.

Áke and Grima discover Aslaug by Mårten Eskil Winge, 1862

They named her Kráka (Crow) and raised her as their own. To avoid suspicion, they hid her beauty and nobility by shaving her head, smearing her in tar, and dressing her in a long hood.

Years later when she was bathing, she was discovered by some of King Ragnar's men. They were so entranced by her beauty that they burned the bread they were making. When Ragnar asked them how this happened, and he learned of her beauty he sent for the young woman. To test her character he commanded her to arrive neither dressed nor undressed, neither fasting nor eating, and neither alone nor in company. Kráka arrived dressed in a net, biting a leek, and with a dog as a companion. Ragnar was impressed by her ingenuity and found her to be a wise companion. He proposed marriage to her, but she refused until he accomplished his mission in Norway.

There are motifs in this story that are common in folklore and mythology in many different traditions, matching the Aarne-Thompson-Uther Index (ATU) number 875, 'Clever Peasant Girl', and the Brothers Grimm tale 'Die kluge Bauerntochter' or 'The Peasant's Wise Daughter'.

Kráka warned Ragnar to wait three nights until their marriage could be consummated, but Ragnar could not wait and insisted on sleeping with her immediately after the wedding, contrary to her advice, and their first son Ivar was born weak, or "boneless". Their sons Bjorn 'Ironside', Halfdan 'Hvitserk', and Rognvald soon followed.

Ragnar and his men attended a feast of King Eystein at Uppsala, who had a beautiful daughter called Ingibjorg. Ragnar's men proposed that Ragnar should be betrothed to Ingibjorg and no longer be with Kráka, who they all believed was a mere peasant's daughter. On their return, Ragnar instructed his men on pain of death to say nothing of the betrothal to King Eystein's daughter. Kráka persistently asked Ragnar what news he brought back with him, but he said he knew of no news to tell, and later claimed to be tired and sleepy after his return journey.

Kráka revealed to Ragnar that she knew all about the betrothal, not because any of his men disobeyed him, but because she was told by three birds who sat in the tree beside where the betrothal was made, revealing that she was a völva, a seeress with supernatural powers of prophecy. She then revealed that she was not a peasant's daughter, but actually Aslaug, the daughter of Sigurd the slayer of the dragon Fafnir, and the shield-maiden Brynhild the daughter of Budla, and news of her identity and lineage was spread to every man in the land.

Aslaug revealed that she was with child, and prophecised that it would be a boy with a birth mark that will look like a serpent in his eyes. She advised him that if her prophecy was correct, he should not go to Sweden or marry King Eystein's daughter. Sigurd Snake-in-the-eyes was born.

Ragnar's eldest sons with Thora Borgarhjört: Erik and Agnarr, waged war against King Eystein. Agnarr fell in battle, and Erik asked to be put to death on a bed of spears. Upon learning this news, Aslaug shed tears of blood.

Aslaug and Ragnar's sons planned to avenge Erik and Agnarr's death, and Aslaug briefly changed her name to Randalin. They were successful in overcoming King Eystein's sorcery and his possessed cow Sibilja who was feared for her charging and bellowing. They defeated them both and achieved great fame.

When Ragnar learned of his sons' success, he hoped to achieve something equally great by conquering England with only two large ships. Aslaug advised him that it was a bad idea, but he decided to go anyway:

> *"Mér sýnist sjá eigi minni fékostnaðr, áðr þessi skip sé búin, en þótt þú hefðir langskip mörg til þessarar ferðar.*
>
> *En þú veist þat, at illt er skipum at halda at Englandi, ok ef svá verðr, at skip þín týndist, þótt menn komist á land, þá eru þeir þegar upp gefnir, ef landherr kemr at, en betra er at halda langskipum til hafna en knörrum".*[15]

> "It seems to me no less expensive, instead of building these ships, for you to have many longships for that kind of journey.
>
> But you know that it is bad for ships to sail for England, and if it happens that your ship is wrecked, though many come to land, then they must surrender straight away, if the lord of the land comes, then it is better to have longships in the harbour than knorrs".

Ragnar was defeated and captured by King Ælla of Northumbria, where he was thrown into a snake pit to die. Aslaug and Ragnar's sons avenged Ragnar's death by forming the Great Heathen Army, invading England, and killing King Ælla by 'blood eagle'. Aslaug (Randalin) lived to old age, and learned of the death of her son Hvitserk, who was killed while raiding in eastern lands, and the death of her son Sigurd Snake-in-the-eye, whose daughter she fostered giving her the same name as her.

The fact that Aslaug has three names throughout these sagas indicates a possible blending of history, legend, and mythology. Perhaps this is in part to connect Ragnar Lothbrok back to mythology, adding gravity and legitimacy to his legend, and also to those who later claimed to be descended from him.

---

[15] Embleton, M. L. (Translator), Ragnars Saga Loðbrókar (The Saga of Ragnar Lothbrok):, The Sagas of Ragnar Lothbrok: Norse Text, Translation, and Word List, 2nd Ed., 2021, London, Independent, 2021, p.65, ISBN 979-8475152591

5.   The Sons of Ragnar Lothbrok

5.1.   Erik 'Weatherhat' Ragnarsson

Erik 'Weatherhat' with his army by Olaus Magnus, c1555

Erik 'Weatherhat' was a legendary king of Sweden, who according to the Swedish Chronicles earned his nickname because he always enjoyed favourable winds while raiding in the Baltic Sea, using the power of his hat to change the winds in his favour. In Saxo's *Gesta Danorum*, Erik 'Weatherhat' is linked with Eirk Ragnarsson. When Ragnar took his sons Bjorn, Fridlief, and Ragbard with him to defeat Sorle and secure his sons' inheritance, Erik, one of his sons with Aslaug (Swanloga) was not yet old enough to bear arms. Once Sorle was defeated, Ragnar then appointed Erik to rule over Sweden:

"Regnaldus, Withsercus et Ericus, quos ex Suanlogha progenuerat, nondum habilem armis aetatem impleverant - Suetiam petiit".[16]

"Ragnald, Hvitserk, and Erik, who of Swanloga (Aslaug) were born, had not yet had the age of bearing arms, and went to Sweden".

"Inde profectus filium suum Ericum, Ventosi Pillei cognomen habentem, Suetiae praefert".[17]

"Then appointed son his Erik, Wind-Hat the name he had, over Sweden as he preferred".

Ragnar later summoned Erik to go raiding with him in the Orkneys to suppress a Scottish rebellion:

"Deinde, eo atque Erico accitis, Orcades populatus, ad ultimum Scotorum finibus appulit eorumque regem Murial triduano exhaustum proelio interfecit".[18]

"Then he summoned him Erik, and ravaged the Orkneys, landed at last of the territory of the Scots, and in three days of battle wearied out their king Murial, and slew him".

---

[16] Saxo Grammaticus, Gesta Danorum: Saxonis Grammatici Danorum Historiae Libri XVI, 1534, Switzerland, Universitätsbibliothek Basel, 2010, p.203 <https://www.e-rara.ch/bau_1/content/zoom/889580> Accessed 25/11/2021

[17] Saxo Grammaticus, p. 207

[18] Saxo Grammaticus, p. 207

Erik's brother Agnarr later learned that Erik had been slain in Sweden at the hands of Osten (Eystein), and vowed to avenge his death, but was defeated in battle:

"Post haec Ericum apud Suetiam Osteni cuiusdam malignitate sublatum ulcisci cupiens, dum alienae vindictae artius incumbit, suum hosti sanguinem erogavit, dumque caesi fratris poenas avidius expetit, proprium fraternae caritati funus impendit".[19]

"After these things, Erik was taken in Sweden by the malice of a certain Osten, desiring to take revenge, while the revenge of another is most closely pressed, he laid out his blood for the enemy, while he eagerly sought the punishment of his brother's slaying, for the love of his brother his death is paid out".

In *Ragnars Saga Loðbrókar* he is not given the nickname 'Weatherhat'. Erik and his younger brother Agnarr are the two sons of Ragnar Lothbrok and Thora Borgarhjört, who grew up to be strong and famous warriors:

"Nú eru þeir Eirekr ok Agnarr, synir Ragnars, miklir menn fyrir sér, svá at trautt finnast þeira jafningjar, ok búa þeir á herskipum hvert sumar ok eru ágætir af sínum hernaði".[20]

"Now Ragnar's sons Erik and Agnarr, were such great mighty men, that their equal could not be found, they prepared their ships each summer and were renowned for their raiding".

When Ragnar broke off his betrothal to Swedish King Eystein's daughter Ingibjorg, their friendship was ended. Sensing the coming hostilities, Erik and Agnarr decided to attack:

"Ok þá er þeir Eirekr ok Agnarr, synir Ragnars, spyrja þetta, þá ræddu þeir með sér, at þeir mundu fá sér lið mikit, sem þeir mætti mest, ok mundu herja á Svíþjóð".[21]

"And then when Ragnar's sons Erik and Agnarr learned of this, they decided among themselves that they would get themselves the greatest company that they could, and they would wage war in Sweden".

Erik and Agnarr and their company faced the larger numbers of King Eystein's forces, and their sorcery in the form of a cow called Sibilja, who shrieked and bellowed and gored many men.

When Erik saw that his younger brother Agnarr had fallen in battle, it made him fight even harder, no longer caring what happened to him. He was eventually captured and carried. Even though King Eystein offered him mercy, and the hand of his daughter Ingibjorg, Erik refused a life of defeat, instead choosing death by being sacrificed on a bed of spears, while his men were given mercy and set free.

---

[19] Saxo Grammaticus, Gesta Danorum: Saxonis Grammatici Danorum Historiae Libri XVI, 1534, Switzerland, Universitätsbibliothek Basel, 2010, p.209 <https://www.e-rara.ch/bau_1/content/zoom/889580> Accessed 25/11/2021
[20] Embleton, M. L. (Translator), Ragnars Saga Loðbrókar (The Saga of Ragnar Lothbrok):, The Sagas of Ragnar Lothbrok: Norse Text, Translation, and Word List, 2nd Ed., 2021, London, Independent, 2021, p.31, ISBN 979-8475152591
[21] Embleton, M. L., 2021, p.41

When Aslaug learned of the deaths of Erik and Agnarr, she shed tears of blood. With much discussion and planning, Aslaug and Ragnar's sons defeated King Eystein and his sorcery and avenged Erik and Agnarr's deaths, earning great fame.

In *Ragnarssona Þáttr* the hostility between brothers Erik and Agnarr and King Eystein of Sweden was because of Erik and Agnarr's request of transfer of King Eystein's tribute from Ragnar to them, which was rejected by King Eystein and all of his chieftains:

> *"Ok er þeir fundust, sagði Eiríkr, at hann vildi, at Eysteinn konungr heldi Svíaríki undir þá bræðr, ok kveðst þá fá vilja Borghildar, dóttur hans, ok segir, at þá megu þeir vel halda því ríki fyrir Ragnari konungi".*[22]

> "And when they met, Erik said that he wanted King Eystein to hold Sweden under the brothers, and that he wished to marry his daughter Borghild, and said that then they may well hold the kingdom for King Ragnar".

Another difference is that in the *Gesta Danorum*, Erik and Agnarr are the sons of Aslaug (*Swanloga*), and they die against the same enemy, but at different times, whereas in *Ragnars Saga Loðbrókar* and *Ragnarssona Þáttr*, they are the sons of Thora Borgarhjört, and they both die in the same battle.

Erik 'Weatherhat' is also equated with the semi-legendary Swedish king Erik Anundsson or Eymundsson, who as the name suggests was not one of Ragnar's sons. He ruled Sweden between 880 and 882 and successfully extended his rule around the Baltic Sea, and is mentioned in Hervarar Saga:

> *"Eiríkr hét sonr Önundar konungs, er ríki tók eptir föður sinn at Uppsölum; hann var ríkr konungr. Á hans dögum hófst til ríkis í Noregi Haraldr hárfagri, er fyrstr kom einvaldi í Noreg sinna ættmanna".*[23]

> "Erik was the son of king Anund, and he succeeded his father at Uppsala; he was a rich king. During his reign, Harald Fairhair came to power in Norway, Harald was the first of his kin to reign as a monarch in Norway".

Haralds Saga Hárfagra states that Erik died when Harald Fairhair had been king of all Norway for ten years:

> *"Eiríkr konungr lifði Emundarson; hann andaðisk, þá er Haraldr konungr inn hárfagri hafði verit x. vetr konungr í Nóregi".*[24]

> "Erik the King lived with Edmundarson, he died, then as Harald the King the fair-haired had been 10 winters king of Norway".

---

[22] Embleton, M. L. (Translator), Ragnarssona Þáttr (The Tale of Ragnar's Sons):, The Sagas of Ragnar Lothbrok: Norse Text, Translation, and Word List, 2nd Ed., 2021, London, Independent, 2021, p.94, ISBN 979-8475152591

[23] Hervarar Saga ok Heiðreks (The Saga of Hervör and Heidrek):, 13th Century, Iceland, Netútgáfan (Online Version), 1998, <https://www.snerpa.is/net/index.html> Accessed 13/01/2022

[24] Snorri Sturluson, Heimskringla: Haralds Saga Hárfagra, c1220s, Iceland, Heimskringla.no, 2020, <https://heimskringla.no/wiki/Haraldz_saga_ins_hárfagra_(FJ)> Accessed 13/02/2022

5.2.   Agnarr Ragnarsson

Agnarr is one of the sons of Ragnar Lothbrok. He is mentioned in the *Gesta Danorum*, *Ragnars Saga Loðbrókar* and *Ragnarssona Þáttr*.

In the *Gesta Danorum* Agnarr, one of Ragnar's sons with Aslaug (*Swanloga*), was appointed to rule over England by his brothers Ivar and Siward who returned to Denmark to concentrate on suppressing a revolt by the Danes. The English rejected Agnarr's rule, and he came to despise the country.

"Qui repulsa provocatus Anglorum, opitulante Siwardo, contemptricem sui provinciam incolis vacuefaciendo, tenacia situ iugera cultore carere quam insolentem alere maluit, pinguissimaque insulae rura taeterrima vastitate perfundens desertae quam superbae regioni imperitare satius autumavit".[25]

"Agnarr was repulsed and provoked by the English, and with the help of Siward, had contempt for his province and evacuated it of its tenants, it was deprived of the tenacious tillers of the fields, rather than feeding its most insolent, and the richest country of the island was laid waste, which he thought better than ruling a proud country".

Agnarr later learned that his brother Erik had been slain in Sweden at the hands of Osten (*Eystein*), and vowed to avenge his death, but was defeated in battle:

"Post haec Ericum apud Suetiam Osteni cuiusdam malignitate sublatum ulcisci cupiens, dum alienae vindictae artius incumbit, suum hosti sanguinem erogavit, dumque caesi fratris poenas avidius expetit, proprium fraternae caritati funus impendit".[26]

"After these things, Erik was taken in Sweden by the malice of a certain Osten, desiring to take revenge, while the revenge of another is most closely pressed, he laid out his blood for the enemy, while he eagerly sought the punishment of his brother's slaying, for the love of his brother his death is paid out".

In *Ragnars Saga Loðbrókar*, Agnarr and his older brother Eirek were the two sons of Ragnar Lothbrok and Thora Borgarhjört, who grew up to be strong and famous warriors:

"Nú eru þeir Eirekr ok Agnarr, synir Ragnars, miklir menn fyrir sér, svá at trautt finnast þeira jafningjar, ok búa þeir á herskipum hvert sumar ok eru ágætir af sínum hernaði".[27]

"Now Ragnar's sons Erik and Agnarr, were such great mighty men, that their equal could not be found, they prepared their ships each summer and were renowned for their raiding".

---

[25] Saxo Grammaticus, Gesta Danorum: Saxonis Grammatici Danorum Historiae Libri XVI, 1534, Switzerland, Universitätsbibliothek Basel, 2010, p.209 <https://www.e-rara.ch/bau_1/content/zoom/889580> Accessed 25/11/2021

[26] Saxo Grammaticus, p.209

[27] Embleton, M. L. (Translator), Ragnars Saga Loðbrókar (The Saga of Ragnar Lothbrok):, The Sagas of Ragnar Lothbrok: Norse Text, Translation, and Word List, 2nd Ed., 2021, London, Independent, 2021, p.31, ISBN 979-8475152591

When Ragnar broke off his betrothal to Swedish King Eystein's daughter Ingibjorg, their friendship was ended. Sensing the coming hostilities, Erik and Agnarr decided to attack:

"Ok þá er þeir Eirekr ok Agnarr, synir Ragnars, spyrja þetta, þá ræddu þeir með sér, at þeir mundu fá sér lið mikit, sem þeir mætti mest, ok mundu herja á Svíþjóð".[28]

"And then when Ragnar's sons Erik and Agnarr learned of this, they decided among themselves that they would get themselves the greatest company that they could, and they would wage war in Sweden".

Erik and Agnarr and their company faced the larger numbers of King Eystein's forces, and their sorcery in the form of a cow called Sibilja, who shrieked and bellowed and gored many men. Eventually Agnarr was killed in battle:

"Þeir Eirekr ok Agnarr váru í öndverðri fylkingu þann dag, ok opt gengu þeir í gegnum fylkingar Eysteins konungs.

Ok nú fell Agnarr".

"Erik and Agnarr were in at the front of the ranks that day, and they often went among and through King Eystein's ranks.

And now Agnarr fell".

When Erik saw that his younger brother Agnarr had fallen in battle, it made him fight even harder, no longer caring what happened to him. He was eventually captured and carried.

Even though King Eystein offered him mercy, and the hand of his daughter Ingibjorg, Erik refused a life of defeat, instead choosing death by being sacrificed on a bed of spears, while his men were given mercy and set free.

When Aslaug learned of the deaths of Erik and Agnarr, she shed tears of blood. With much discussion and planning, Aslaug and Ragnar's sons defeated King Eystein and his sorcery and avenged Erik and Agnarr's deaths, earning great fame.

In *Ragnarssona Þáttr* the hostility between brothers Erik and Agnarr and King Eystein of Sweden was because of Erik and Agnarr's request of transfer of King Eystein's tribute from Ragnar to them, which was rejected by King Eystein and all of his chieftains:

"Ok er þeir fundust, sagði Eiríkr, at hann vildi, at Eysteinn konungr heldi Svíaríki undir þá bræðr, ok kveðst þá fá vilja Borghildar, dóttur hans, ok segir, at þá megu þeir vel halda því ríki fyrir Ragnari konungi".

"And when they met, Erik said that he wanted King Eystein to hold Sweden under the brothers, and that he wished to marry his daughter Borghild, and said that then they may well hold the kingdom for King Ragnar".

Another difference is that in the *Gesta Danorum*, Erik and Agnarr are the sons of Aslaug (*Swanloga*), and they die against the same enemy, but at different times, whereas in *Ragnars Saga Loðbrókar* and *Ragnarssona Þáttr*, they are the sons of Thora Borgarhjört, and they both die in the same battle.

---

[28] Embleton, M. L. (Translator), Ragnars Saga Loðbrókar (The Saga of Ragnar Lothbrok):, The Sagas of Ragnar Lothbrok: Norse Text, Translation, and Word List, 2nd Ed., 2021, London, Independent, 2021, p.41, ISBN 979-8475152591

5.3.   Bjorn 'Ironside' Ragnarsson

Bjorn Ironside (*Bjǫrn Járnsíða*) was a chieftain and a legendary king of Sweden, and one of the sons of Ragnar Lothbrok.

According to the *Gesta Danorum*, Bjorn was given the nickname 'Ironside' or 'Ironsides' on account of his success on the battlefield without any injury to himself, as if his sides had the firmness of iron.

> *"Biornus vero, quod integer hosti cladem ingesserat, tamquam a ferrei lateris firmitate sempiternum usurpavit agnomen".*[29]

> "But Biornus, because he had inflicted complete defeat on the enemy, as if from the firmness of iron brick he used the nickname forever".

According to William of Jumièges in his *Gesta Normannorum Ducum*, Bjorn Ironside (*Bier Costae Ferrae*) the son of Ragnar Lothbrok (*Lothbroci regis filio*), was ordered to leave his realm, as per the tradition of the times, and Bjorn went raiding in West Francia and then later in the Mediterranean.[30]

He was first mentioned in the *Annales Fontanellenses* in the year 855:

> *"Anno 855 indictione 3 ipso die 15 kalend Augusti,*
>
> *maxima classis Danorum fluvium Sequanae occupat, duce item Sydroc, et usque Pistis castrum"…*
> …*"Deinde post dies 33, id est 14 Kalend Septembris,*
>
> *Berno Nortmannus cum valida classe ingressus est. Deinde iunctis viribus"…*
>
> …*"maxima eos strage percussit".*[31]

> "In the year 855, the 3rd indiction, on the 15th day before the Kalends of August (18th July),
>
> the largest fleet of Danes the river Seine occupied, led also by Sigtrygg, and up to Pîtres encamped"...
> …"Then after 33 days, that is the 14th day before the Kalends of September (19th August),
>
> Berno (Bjorn), the Northman with a powerful fleet entered. Then, having joined forces"…
>
> …"the greatest of them carnage struck".

Sigtrygg left the next year, but Bjorn received reinforcements from another army and further established himself in the Seine area.

---

[29] Saxo Grammaticus, Gesta Danorum: Saxonis Grammatici Danorum Historiae Libri XVI, 1534, Switzerland, Universitätsbibliothek Basel, 2010, p.203 <https://www.e-rara.ch/bau_1/content/zoom/889580> Accessed 25/11/2021

[30] Guillaume de Jumiège, Gesta Normannorum Ducum (Deeds of the Dukes of Normandy), 1060: pub. pour la première fois en français par M. Guizot, et suivie de la Vie de Guillaume-le-conquérant, par Guillaume de Poitiers, 1826, Paris, Hathitrust Digital Library, 2019, p.11-13 <https://babel.hathitrust.org/cgi/pt?id=mdp.39015013753564&view=1up&seq=23&skin=2021> Accessed 22/11/2021

[31] Pertz, Georg Heinrich (Ed.), Annales Fontanellenses (Annals of Fontanelle), 855:, 1829, Hannover & Leipzig, Die digitalen Monumenta Germaniae Historica (dMGH), 2004, p.304 <https://web.archive.org/web/20181203055459/https://www.dmgh.de/de/fs1/object/display/bsb00000869_00325.html> Accessed 22/11/2021

They later set up camp for the winter at a place known as Givold's Fosse (Jeufosse), on a bend of the river between Vernon and Bonnières.

From this base they launched an attack on Paris from the end of 856 to the beginning of 857, and constructed a fort at the island of Oissel (*Oscellus*) near Rouen.

In the year 858 the *Annales Bertiniani* recorded a treaty between Charles the Bald and the Seine Vikings, in which Bjorn swore fealty to Charles.

At the same time another faction of Bjorn's forces kidnapped abbot Ludwig of Saint Dionysus and his brother in return for a large ransom paid in treasures:

"Berno, dux partis piratarum Sequanae insistentium, ad Karlum regem in Vermeria palatio venit,	"Berno, the leader of the party of the pirates of the Seine, came to King Charles in the palace of Vermeria,
eiusque se manibus dedens, fidelitatem statim iurat.	he surrendered his hands, and immediately swore fealty.
Pars altera eorundem piratarum Hludowicum, abbatem monaeterii Sancti Dyonysii cum fratre ipsius Gauzleno capiunt,	Another part of the same pirates, Ludwig, abbot of the Monastery of Saint Dionysius with his brother Gauzlenus captured,
eisque redemptionis suae gravissimam multam imponunt, ob quam multi thesaurorum ecclesiarum Dei ex regno Karli, ipso iubente exhausti sunt;	·for their redemption a great burden imposed, of which many treasures of the church of God and King Charles were exhausted by the command;
sed his minime sufficientibus, ab eodem rege et omnibus episcopis, abbatibus, comitibus ceterisque viris potentibus multa ad suppletionem praedictae summae certatim conlata sunt".[32]	but these not being sufficient, at the same time the king and all the bishops, abbots, companions, and the rest of the powerful did much to supplement the aforementioned sum they struggled to complete".

Bjorn's name did not appear again in contemporary sources after 858, but the Seine Vikings continued their raiding for several years, attacking Paris again in 861.

According to William of Jumièges in his *Gesta Normannorum Ducum*, Bjorn was fostered by the Viking chieftan Hastein. Bjorn and one or more of his brothers joined Hastein in raiding in the Mediterranean.

They attacked the town of Luni in Italy, believing it to be Rome, and eventually gained entry, but when they realised however that Luni was not in fact Rome, and heard that Rome was well prepared for defence, they returned to West Europe and parted company with Hastein.

On his way back Bjorn was apparently shipwrecked on the English coast and barely survived, making his way across the English Channel to Frisia, where he died, according to William of Jumièges. This version of events conflicts with other sources which state that Bjorn ruled in Uppsala, Sweden.

In *Ragnars Saga Loðbrókar*, Bjorn is the son of Ragnar and Aslaug, along with his brothers Hvitserk, Ivar the Boneless, and Sigurd Snake-in-the-eye.

---

[32] Waitz, Georg (Ed.), Annales Bertiniani (Annals of Saint Bertin), 858: MGH SS 1, 1826, Hannover & Leipzig, Die digitalen Monumenta Germaniae Historica (dMGH), 2004, p.451
<https://www.dmgh.de/mgh_ss_1/index.htm#page/451/mode/1up> Accessed 22/11/2021

Bjorn also had two half brothers Erik and Agnarr from Ragnar's previous marriage with Thora Borgarhjört. Bjorn and his brothers left Sweden to conquer Zealand, Jutland, Gotland, Öland and all the minor islands, eventually settling at Lejre in Zealand, Denmark with Ivar the Boneless as their leader.

On learning of the death of his half brothers Erik and Agnarr at the hands of King Eystein of Sweden, Bjorn and his brothers sailed to Sweden with a large army.

Their mother Aslaug (who changed her name to Randalin) rode with a cavalry over land to join them, and together they defeated King Eystein in spite of his sorcery, and achieved great fame.

Later learning of the death of his father Ragnar at the hands of King Ælla in England, Bjorn and his brothers attempted to avenge his death by attacking King Ælla, but they were unsuccessful and driven back.

Bjorn's brother Ivar the Boneless sought reconciliation with King Ælla and gained land in England, which he used as a base to become more and more popular in England, gradually diverting the loyalty and support of the English chieftains to himself and out from under King Ælla.

When Bjorn and his brothers raised the Great Heathen Army, they had the greater numbers due to the shift in loyalties to Ivar the Boneless, and King Ælla was defeated and killed by blood eagle.

Later Bjorn and his brothers raided in England, Normandy, France, and Lombardy, on their way to Luna in Italy:

> *"Nú ætla þeir at létta eigi fyrr en þeir koma til Rómaborgar, af því at sú borg var þeim bæði sögð mikil ok fjölmenn ok ágæt ok auðig.*
> *En þat vissu þeir eigi gerla, hvé löng leið þangat er, en þeir höfðu svá mikit lið, at eigi fengust vistir".[33]*

> "They intended not to rest until they came to the city of Rome, for they were told that this city was great, and populous, and famous, and wealthy.
> But they did not know completely, how long the journey was from there, and they had so many men, that provisions could not be obtained".

They were then met by a kindly old man who described himself as a beggar and a lifelong traveller. Bjorn and his brothers were keen to learn what they could from the old man and asked him how far the journey was to Rome:

> *"Hann svarar: "Ek kann segja yðr nokkut til merkja.*
> *Þér meguð hér sjá þessa járnskó, er ek hefi á fótum mér, þeir eru nú fornir, ok þá aðra, er ek hefi á baki mér, þeir eru nú ok slitnir.*

> "He answered: "I can say to you something of a sign.
> You may see here these iron shoes, that I have on my feet, they are now old, and the others, that I have on my back, they are now also broken.

---

[33] Embleton, M. L. (Translator), Ragnars Saga Loðbrókar (The Saga of Ragnar Lothbrok):, The Sagas of Ragnar Lothbrok: Norse Text, Translation, and Word List, 2nd Ed., 2021, London, Independent, 2021, p.62, ISBN 979-8475152591

En þá er ek fór þaðan, batt ek þessa á fætr mér ina slitnu, er ek hefi nú á baki mér, ok váru þá nýir báðir, ok á þeiri leið hefi ek verit ávallt síðan".

About the time when I travelled from there, I bought these for my feet which are broken now on my back, they were both new, and I have been on that journey ever since".

En er inn gamli maðr hafði þetta mælt, þykkjast þeir sjá, at þeir megu eigi þessu á leið koma, er þeir hafa fyrir sér ætlat, til Róms at fara". [34]

Then as the old man had said this, they thought it seemed that they may not journey as they had intended before, to Rome".

The sagas then tell that they continued on to raid many other cities which had not been won before, and that there are tokens of their achievements which can still be seen to this day.

When Bjorn and his brothers returned to Scandinavia, all of the kingdoms were divided up between them, and Bjorn ruled at Uppsala in Sweden.

Hervarar Saga tells us that Bjorn had two sons: Refil, and Erik Bjornsson who became the next king of Sweden, and *Eiríks Saga Rauða* mentions the family line of Thord traced back to another of Bjorn's sons Aslak, who was an ancestor of the explorer Thorfin Karlsefni.

Bjorn's descendants are believed to be the beginning of the Swedish House of Munsö, which ruled over the Swedes until c1060.

One of Bjorn's descendents was Olof Skotkunung, one of the first kings of Sweden about whom there is substantial knowledge. He was the first king to have ruled over the Swedes and the Geats, and his rule marks the transition between the Viking Age and the Middle Ages in Scandinavia.

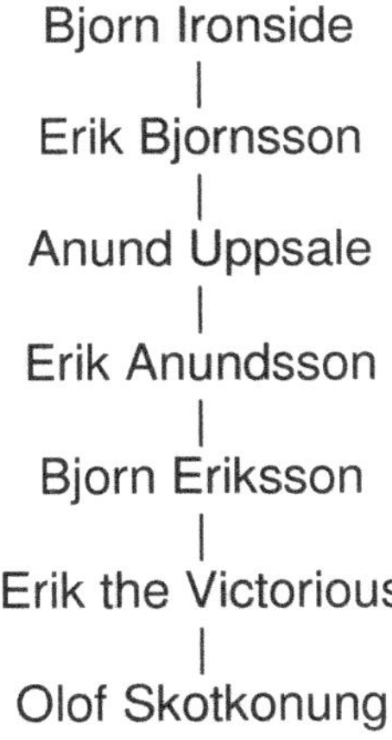

---

[34] Embleton, M. L. (Translator), Ragnars Saga Loðbrókar (The Saga of Ragnar Lothbrok):, The Sagas of Ragnar Lothbrok: Norse Text, Translation, and Word List, 2nd Ed., 2021, London, Independent, 2021, p.63, ISBN 979-8475152591

5.4.   Halfdan 'Hvitserk' Ragnarsson

Halfdan 'Hvitserk' Ragnarsson by Herbert Cole, 1907

Halfdan (*Hálfdan, Halfdene, Healfdene, Albann*) 'Hvitserk' Ragnarsson was one of the sons of Ragnar Lothbrok and Aslaug, along with Ivar the Boneless, Bjorn Ironside, and Rognvald, and two half brothers Erik and Agnarr.

Because the names Halfdan and Hvitserk never appeared together in any sources, it is believed that they are in fact the same person.

Halfdan was a common name in Scandinavia during the Viking Age, and the nickname Hvitserk (white-shirt) distinguished him from others with the same name.

In *Ragnars Saga Loðbrókar* and *Ragnarssona Þáttr*, Halfdan (also called Hvitserk the Swift) took part in a combined attack on King Eystein of Sweden to avenge the death of Erik and Agnarr.

"Nú ganga þeir svá hart fram bræðr, Hvítserkr ok Björn, at engi fylking stendr við.
Ok nú fellr svá mjök lið Eysteins konungs, at minna stendr upp, en sumt kemr á flótta.
Ok nú lýkr svá þeira bardaga, at Eysteinn konungr fellr, en þeir bræðr hafa sigr".[35]

"Now the brothers Hvitserk and Bjorn went forwards so roughly, that none of the ranks could withstand them.
And now so many of King Eystein's forces fell, that few were left standing, and some came to flee.
And now they ended the battle, as King Eystein fell, and the brothers had success".

When Ragnar's sons learned of the death of their father Ragnar, Halfdan grasped a gaming piece in his hand so tightly that blood emanated from each of his finger nails (in the *Gesta Danorum*, it is Bjorn who grasps the dice making his fingers bleed).

---

[35] Embleton, M. L. (Translator), Ragnars Saga Loðbrókar (The Saga of Ragnar Lothbrok):, The Sagas of Ragnar Lothbrok: Norse Text, Translation, and Word List, 2nd Ed., 2021, London, Independent, 2021, p.57, ISBN 979-8475152591

> *"En Hvítserkr hélt töfl einni, er hann hafði drepit, ok hann kreisti hana svá fast, at blóð stökk undan hverjum nagli".[36]*

> "Then Hvitserk held a game piece in his hand, and he crushed it so tightly that blood emanated from each nail".

Gripped with rage, Halfdan he was quick to suggest that they avenge his death immediately by killing the messengers who have been sent to them, but this idea was rejected by Ivar the Boneless, whom the brothers trusted as the wisest among them in all decisions.

Ivar sought reconciliation with King Ælla and gained land in England, which he used as a base to become more and more popular in England, gradually diverting the loyalty and support of the English chieftains to himself and out from under King Ælla.

When Halfdan and his brothers raised the Great Heathen Army, they had the greater numbers due to the shift in loyalties to Ivar the Boneless, and King Ælla was defeated and killed by blood eagle.

After further raiding along the Mediterranean and in Italy, Halfdan and his brothers returned to Scandinavia, and all of the kingdoms were divided up between them.

Halfdan ruled in Jutland and Wendland, and raided widely in France with his brothers Bjorn Ironside and Sigurd Snake-in-the-eye.

Later Halfdan's mother Aslaug, who changed her name to Randalin, was an old woman when she learned of Halfdan's death while raiding in eastern lands:

> *"En Randalín, móðir þeira, varð gömul kona.*
> *En Hvítserkr, sonr hennar, hafði herjat eitthvert sinn í Austrveg, ok kom svá mikit ofrefli í mót honum, at hann mátti eigi rönd við reisa, ok varð hann handtekinn.*
> *En hann kaus sér þann dauðdaga, at bál skyldi gera af mannahöfðum; þar skyldi hann brenna, ok svá lét hann líf sitt".[37]*

> "Then Randalin, their mother, was an old woman.
> Then Hvitserk, her son, had raided some eastern lands, and such overwhelming forces came against him, that he would not withstand then, and he was captured.
> But he chose his own death day, that a fire should be made of men's heads burning, and so he lay down his life there".

These eastern lands are believed to be Gardarike (*Garðaríki*), the old norse term used in medieval times for the states of the Keivan Rus', a group of Slavic, Baltic, and Finnic peoples in Eastern and Northern Europe that later became parts of Belarus, Russia, and Ukraine.

Other accounts differ with the sagas and give a more detailed account of Halfdan's activities with the Great Heathen Army.

He became the main commander of the army in 870 and invaded Wessex, battling the West Saxons nine times without being able to defeat them.

---

[36] Embleton, M. L. (Translator), Ragnars Saga Loðbrókar (The Saga of Ragnar Lothbrok):, The Sagas of Ragnar Lothbrok: Norse Text, Translation, and Word List, 2nd Ed., 2021, London, Independent, 2021, p.73, ISBN 979-8475152591
[37] Embleton, M. L., p.83

The army then retreated to the captured town of London, and coins minted in London during this period identify Halfdan as its leader.

In 872 the army moved north to Northumbria, supposedly to quell a revolt against their puppet king Ecgberht, or possibly because of a war with the Kingdom of Mercia.

Wintering at Torksey in Lincolnshire, and then Repton in Derbyshire, the army then conquered Mercia in 874, deposing the Mercian king Burghred and replacing him with the puppet king Ceolwulf.

The army then split in two, with one half under Guthrum heading south to fight against Wessex, the other half under Halfdan heading north to fight against the Picts and Britons of Strathclyde.

The *Annals of Ulster* in 875 mentioned Eystein (*Oistín*) Olafsson being deceitfully killed by Albann, who is believed to be Halfdan.

> *"Oistin m. Amlaiph regis Norddmannorum ab Alband per dolum occisus est".*[38]

> "Oistín son of Amlaíb, king of the Norsemen, was deceitfully killed by Albann".

Halfdan's activity in Ireland was an attempt to regain the kingdom that his brother Ivar had gained before his death in 873. He returned to Northumbria where he became King of York (*Jórvík*) in 876.

While Halfdan was away in York, his rule of Dublin was deposed. He returned to Ireland in 877 to try and retake the throne, but he was met with an army of 'fair heathens' led by Bárid mac Ímair (*Bárðr*) king of Dublin.

The term 'fair heathens' was used to describe the Norse people or Vikings that had been in Ireland the longest, as opposed to the 'dark heathens' who had arrived more recently, which included Halfdan himself.

The forces met at the Battle of Strangford Lough in 877 where Halfdan was slain in battle. Bárid mac Ímair was wounded in action, but continued to rule Dublin until 881.

Halfdan's forces were defeated and those who survived returned to Northumbria via Scotland.

There is some disagreement among historians about the status of Halfdan and his brothers as historical figures, and their relation to each other.

The degree to which they are related depends on whether all of the brothers are the sons of the same Ragnar in history.

---

[38] Annals of Ulster: MS. Rawl. B. 489, 16th Century, Ireland, Bodleian Library, 2019, f26r <https://digital.bodleian.ox.ac.uk/objects/a5918f5a-2149-47bb-857e-0792bab8085a/surfaces/f0da7984-11aa-419f-ab5d-16efb5c0622b/> Accessed 17/01/2022

5.5.   Ivar 'the Boneless' Ragnarsson

Ivar 'the Boneless' Ragnarsson (*Ívarr hinn Beinlausi*) was a legendary Viking leader who invaded England as part of the Great Heathen Army in 865. He was one of the sons of Ragnar Lothbrok and Aslaug, and his brothers included Bjorn Ironside, Halfdan 'Hvitserk' Ragnarsson, Sigurd Snake-in-the-eye, and Ubba. There are many different spellings of his name in historical sources: *Hingwar, Hyngwar, Imar, Ímar, Inguar, Ingvar, Ingwar, Ivar, Ívar, Ívarr, Ywar,* etc.

Ívarr and Ubba, fol. 48r, MS Harley 2278, British Library, c15th century

The origin of his nickname is explained in *Ragnars Saga Loðbrókar*. Kráka (Aslaug) warned Ragnar to wait three nights until their marriage could be consummated, but Ragnar could not wait and insisted on sleeping with her immediately after the wedding, contrary to her advice, and their first son Ivar was born weak, or "boneless".

"En Kráka kennir sér sóttar ok verðr léttari ok elr sveinbarn, ok var sveinninn vatni ausinn ok nafn gefit ok kallaðr Ívarr.
En sá sveinn var beinlauss ok sem brjósk væri þar, sem bein skyldu vera".[39]

"Then Kraka knew her symptoms and became with child, and raised a baby boy, and the boy was sprinkled with water and given the name Ivar.
But the boy was boneless, as if there was cartilage where bone should be".

When Ivar's half brothers Erik and Agnarr waged war against King Eystein of Sweden, Agnarr fell in battle, and Erik asked to be put to death on a bed of spears. Ivar and his brothers planned to avenge their deaths, and Aslaug briefly changed her name to Randalin. They were successful in overcoming King Eystein's sorcery and his cow named Sibilja, defeating them both in battle and achieving great

---

[39] Embleton, M. L. (Translator), Ragnars Saga Loðbrókar (The Saga of Ragnar Lothbrok):, The Sagas of Ragnar Lothbrok: Norse Text, Translation, and Word List, 2nd Ed., 2021, London, Independent, 2021, p.30, ISBN 979-8475152591

fame. Ivar appears to have employed some sorcery of his own, perhaps aided by Aslaug (Randalin), this included a bow that appeared as weak as a twig, but was then seen to fire arrows that flew as if "shot from the strongest lock bow". Also, Ivar asked to be thrown towards Sibilja the cow, and at first he appeared as light as a child, and then when he landed upon the cow, he became as heavy as a boulder.

When Ragnar learned of his sons' success, he hoped to achieve something equally great by conquering England with only two large ships. Aslaug advised him that it was a bad idea, but he decided to go anyway. Ragnar was defeated and captured by King Ælla of Northumbria, where he was thrown into a snake pit to die.

Ivar was also cunning, and a master of strategy and tactics in battle, playing the longer game in contrast to his hot tempered brothers. For example, when Ivar and his brothers learned of the death of their father Ragnar, Halfdan 'Hvitserk' suggested gaining immediate revenge by killing the messengers who had been sent to them. Ivar dissuaded them from taking such action, having the beginnings of another type of revenge forming in his mind.

Ivar then sought compensation and reconciliation with King Ælla, which his brothers vehemently opposed, thinking it to be a shameful response. Nevertheless, Ivar petitioned the king as follows:

"Ek vil", segir Ívarr, "at þú gefir mér þat af landi þínu, er uxahúð tekr yfir, en þar utan um skal grundvöll gera, ok mun ek eigi til meira mæla við þik, ok þat sé ek, at þú vilt mér engrar sæmdar unna, ef þú vilt eigi þetta".[40]

"I wish", said Ivar, "for you to give me land of yours, that an ox hide may span over, and around that I shall build foundations, and I will not ask any more of you than this, and this I know, you will not grant me any honour, if you will not do this".

Ivar had a bull hide softened and stretched three times, then carved as thin as possible, then split at the hairy and fleshy sides, and then carved into a thin strand that was so long that the area it encircled became London according to *Ragnars Saga Loðbrókar*, or York according to *Ragnarssona Þáttr*. Thus Ivar gained a foothold of land, which he used as a base to become more and more popular in England, gradually diverting the loyalty and support of the English chieftains to himself and out from under King Ælla. His brothers gradually came to realise that this had all been part of a plan to pave the way for a greater revenge.

When Bjorn and his brothers raised the Great Heathen Army, they had the greater numbers due to the shift in loyalties to Ivar the Boneless, and King Ælla was defeated and killed by blood eagle. After this Ivar said to his brothers that he was happy for them to share all the kingdoms among themselves, and that he would rule over England.

In around the year 873 he became gravely ill, and asked to be buried in a place where an invasion might be expected, and predicted that anyone who invaded and came to where he was would be unsuccessful and fall there. His prophecy proved true with Harald 'Hardrada' Sigurdsson who fell thereabouts years later, and when William the Bastard (William the Conqueror) came to land, he broke Ivar's mound and saw that Ivar was un-decayed. He then had Ivar burnt on a pyre, and after that fought for the land and conquered it.

---

[40] Embleton, M. L. (Translator), Ragnars Saga Loðbrókar (The Saga of Ragnar Lothbrok):, The Sagas of Ragnar Lothbrok: Norse Text, Translation, and Word List, 2nd Ed., 2021, London, Independent, 2021, p.78, ISBN 979-8475152591

As well being wise and cunning, Ivar was also noted as being particularly cruel in his persecution of Christians according to some sources. Adam of Bremen (b1050-c1085) was a German historian and chronicler. In his *Gesta Hammaburgensis Ecclesiae Pontificum* (Deeds of the Bishops of Hamburg) he mentions an Ingvar (Ivar) son of Lodparchus (Lothbrok) among those attacking Gallia (West Francia):

"Erant et alii reges Danorum vel Nortmannorun, qui piraticis excursionibus eo tempore Galliam vexabant.
Quorum praecipui erant Horich, Orwig, Gotafrid, Rudolf et Inguar tyranni.
Crudelissimus omnium fuit Inguar, filius Lodparchi, qui christianos ubique per supplicia necavit. Scriptum est in Gestis Francorum".[41]

"They were also other kings of the Danes or of the Northmen, whose pirate excursions at that time Gaul attacked.
The chief of these were Horik, Orwig, Gotafrid, Rudolf and Ingvar, tyrants.
The most cruel of all was Ingvar, the son of Lodparchus, who slew Christians everywhere by torture. It is written in the History of the Franks".

Ivar and his brother Ubba were the leaders of the Danes when they returned to East Anglia in 869. They tortured and killed King Edmund (who would later be known as St Edmund the Martyr) for refusing to renounce Christianity.

The martyrdom of Edmund, Folios 14r and 14v
Passio Sancto Eadmundi, 12th century

[41] Adam of Bremen, Schmeidler, B. (Editor), Gesta Hammaburgensis Ecclesiae Pontificum (Deeds of the Bishops of Hamburg): MGH SS rer. Germ. 2, 3rd Ed., 1917, Hannover & Leipzig, Die digitalen Monumenta Germaniae Historica (dMGH), 2004, p.39
<https://www.dmgh.de/mgh_ss_rer_germ_2/index.htm#page/38/mode/1up> Accessed 17/01/2022

5.6.   Sigurd 'Snake-in-the-eye' Ragnarsson

Sigurd Snake-in-the-eye (*Sigurðr ormr í auga*) was a semi-legendary Viking warrior and Danish king.

He was one of the sons of Ragnar Lothbrok and Aslaug.

His brothers included Bjorn Ironside, Halfdan 'Hvitserk' Ragnarsson, Ivar the Boneless, and Ubba.

In *Ragnars Saga Loðbrókar*, Sigurd's mother Aslaug revealed her noble lineage and prophetic wisdom to Ragnar by predicting that their next son would have a distinctive mark in his eyes.

Left: Sigurd Snake-in-the-eye, from an engraving published by Erico Olai Tormio, 1670

"Hún svarar: "Þú veist, at ek em eigi heill maðr, ok mun þat vera sveinbarn, er ek geng með, en á þeim sveini mun vera þat mark, at svá mun þykkja sem ormr liggi um auga sveininum".[42]

"She answered: "You know that I am with child, and if it should be a baby boy I am walking with, there shall be a mark about his head, that shall look like a serpent lying in the boy's eyes".

The birthmark of a snake lying in or about Sigurd's eyes is believed to be an Ouroboros, an ancient symbol of a snake biting its own tail.

It can be traced from ancient Egyptian iconography, through the Greek magical tradition, and Alchemy.

In some belief systems, this is a prophetic sign that one who encounters or is marked by this symbol has achieved transmigration of the soul, reincarnation, or is destined to achieve fame through all eternity.

Left: An ouroboros drawn by Theodorus Pelecanos, c1478

---

[42] Embleton, M. L. (Translator), Ragnars Saga Loðbrókar (The Saga of Ragnar Lothbrok):, The Sagas of Ragnar Lothbrok: Norse Text, Translation, and Word List, 2nd Ed., 2021, London, Independent, 2021, p.39, ISBN 979-8475152591

Sigurd was three winters old when his half brothers Erik and Agnarr waged war against King Eystein of Sweden. Agnarr fell in battle, and Erik asked to be put to death on a bed of spears.

The family discussed avenging their deaths, and Ivar the Boneless had concerns about King Eystein, who he believed had the gods and magic on his side by practising sorcery and sacrificing to a holy cow called Sibilja.

Next *Ragnars Saga Loðbrókar* tells us that Sigurd spoke a small verse that changed their minds:

"Þat skal þriggja nátta,	"It shall be three nights,
ef þik tregar, móðir,	If you are troubled, mother,
leið eigu vér langa,	Our journey must be long,
leiðangr búinn verða;	For our forces to be ready,
skal Uppsölum eigi,	Uppsala shall not,
þótt ófafé bjóði,	Though wealth offered,
ef oss duga eggjar,	If blade edges aid us,
Eysteinn konungr ráða".[43]	King Eystein rule".

They were successful in overcoming King Eystein's sorcery and his cow named Sibilja, defeating them both in battle and achieving great fame.

When Sigurd and his brothers heard about the death of their father Ragnar, Sigurd was holding a knife in his hand, and was so intent on hearing every detail of the news, that he did not realise that he had cut his hand to the bone.

Bjorn and his brothers attempted to avenge Ragnar's death by attacking King Ælla, but they were unsuccessful and driven back.

Ivar the Boneless sought reconciliation with King Ælla and gained land in England, which he used as a base to become more and more popular in England, gradually diverting the loyalty and support of the English chieftains to himself and out from under King Ælla.

When Sigurd and his brothers raised Great Heathen Army, they had the greater numbers due to the shift in loyalties to Ivar the Boneless, and King Ælla was defeated and killed by blood eagle.

After raiding widely in France and the Mediterranean, the brothers returned to Scandinavia, where all of the kingdoms were divided up between them, and Sigurd inherited Zealand, Scania, Halland, the Danish Islands, and Viken.

It is also possible that Sigurd was co-ruler of Denmark with his brother Halfdan in 873, as Frankish sources mention a Sigfred and Halfdan as rulers. Sigfred and Sigurd are often mixed up in Germanic literature.

When Halfdan died in 877, it is possible that Sigurd ruled in Denmark until he was killed in West Francia in 887.

---

[43] Embleton, M. L. (Translator), Ragnars Saga Loðbrókar (The Saga of Ragnar Lothbrok):, The Sagas of Ragnar Lothbrok: Norse Text, Translation, and Word List, 2nd Ed., 2021, London, Independent, 2021, p.50, ISBN 979-8475152591

5.7.   Ubba Ragnarsson

Ubba (*Ubbi*) Ragnarsson was a Viking and one of the commanders of the Great Heathen Army that invaded England in 865.

Ivar and Ubba setting forth to avenge the death of their father
Fol. 47v, British Library Harley 2278, c15th century

Ubba is not mentioned in *Ragnars Saga Loðbrókar* but according to the *Gesta Danorum*, Ragnar fathered Ubba with an unnamed woman despite the best efforts of her father Esbern (*Hesbernus*) to guard her against such a union.

"Praeterea gignendum ex ea filium sui sanguinis esse, quodque eum Ubbonem nuncupari vellet, adiecit.

Qui cum aliquatenus excrevisset, tenerae aetatis ingenio maturae discretionis habitum apprehendit".[44]

"He further added that the son of his blood had to be begotten by her, and that he wished that he should be called Ubbo.

And when he had grown up to some extent, he possessed the habit of mature discernment by the genius of a tender age".

The Great Heathen Army was made up of various warbands from Scandinavia, Ireland, the Irish Sea, and Frisia. Sources such as the *Historia de Sancto Cuthberto* described Ubba as *dux Fresciorum*, duke or leader of the Frisians, indicating that he was either born there or settled there.

---

[44] Saxo Grammaticus, Gesta Danorum: Saxonis Grammatici Danorum Historiae Libri XVI, 1534, Switzerland, Universitätsbibliothek Basel, 2010, p.204 <https://www.e-rara.ch/bau_1/content/zoom/889580> Accessed 25/11/2021

The Frisians are thought to be the ethnic ancestors of an ancient Germanic tribe called the *Frisii*. The Frisian Kingdom (*Fryske Keninkryk*), also known as *Magna Frisia,* emerged around the year 600 and was at its height around the year 716.

Frisia under the leadership of Redbad (*Radbodo*) in the year 716

After frequent fighting and skirmishes between the Frisians and the Franks, Frisia was defeated at the Battle of the Boarn and absorbed into the Frankish Empire in 734. The Vikings made frequent raids against the Frankish Empire and were granted territory in the area in return for protection from other Viking raids.

The *Anglo-Saxon Chronicle* refers to the Great Heathen Army as '*michel here*' (great army), but the *Historia de Sancto Cuthberto* refers to them as '*Scaldingi*'. One theory is that it means '*Scyldingas*' meaning the descendants of the Danish king Scyld (i.e. Danes).

Another theory is that it means people of the river Scheldt or the island of Walcheren on the river Scheldt, which according to the *Annales Bertiniani* had been granted by Lothair I to a Viking named *Herioldus Iunior* (Harald the Younger) and occupied by Danes since 841.

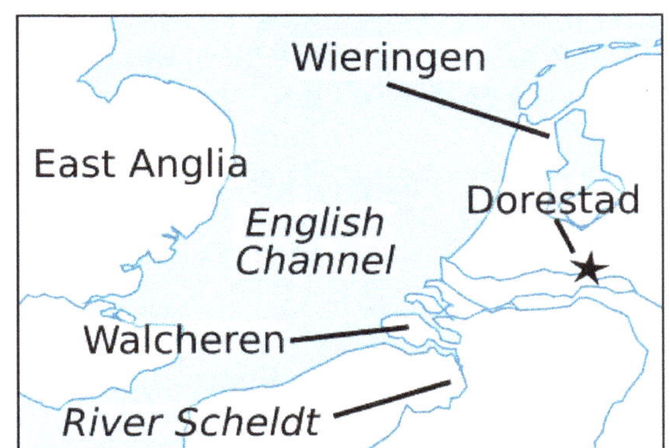

Frisia: Walcheren, the River Scheldt, and Dorestad

Ubba is mentioned in various hagiographies and lives of Anglo-Saxon saints in connection with the Vikings who tortured and killed King Edmund of East Anglia.

St Edmund the Martyr being bound and brought before Ivar
Fol. 28r, Rylands French MS 142, 13th or 14th century

King Edmund later became known as St Edmund the Martyr, and in the cult that grew around him, Ubba and his brother Ivar became archetypal Viking invaders and opponents of Christianity. The *Anglo-Saxon Chronicle* entry for the year 870 reads:

"Her rad se here ofer Mierce innan East Engle and wiñt setl namon. æt Ðeodforda. And þy wint' Eadmund cying him wiþ feaht. and þa Deniscan sige naman þone cyning ofslogon. and þæt lond all ge eodon".[45]	"Here rode the army over Mercia into East Anglia, and winter settling took at Thetford. And that winter Edmund the king they with fought, and the Danish took the victory, and killed the king and that land all they conquered".

In Version F of the *Anglo-Saxon Chronicle* (*Cotton MS Domitian A VIII*), a note can clearly be seen in the right hand margin of the above entry reading "Yngwar *7* Ubbe" (Ivar and Ubba). This note was possibly made in the 16th century by scholar and scribe Robert Talbot (d. 1558), confirming and clarifying that it was Ubba and Ivar who had killed King Edmund.

In *Ragnarssona Þáttr*, after the sons of Ragnar defeated and killed King Ælla by blood eagle, they tortured and killed "King Edmund the Holy" at Ivar's order:

"Eptir þessa orrostu gerðist Ívarr konungr yfir þeim hluta Englands, sem hans frændr höfðu fyrri átt. Hann átti þá tvá bræðr frilluborna, en annarr hét Yngvarr, en annarr Hústó.	"After this battle Ivar made himself king over those parts of England as his kinsmen had before. He then had two brothers bastard born, and one was called Yngvarr, and another Husto.
Þeir pínuðu Játmund konung inn helga eptir boði Ívars, ok lagði hann síðan undir sik hans ríki".[46]	They tortured King Edmund the holy after Ivar's orders, and afterwards he took his kingdom from under him".

---

[45] Anglo-Saxon Chronicle (F, The Bilingual Canterbury Epitome), 870: Cotton MS Domitian A VIII, ff 30r-70v 2021, 11th Century, London, British Library, 2012, f18r <http://www.bl.uk/manuscripts/Viewer.aspx?ref=cotton_ms_tiberius_a_vi_f018r> Accessed 19/01/2022

[46] Embleton, M. L. (Translator), Ragnarssona Þáttr (The Tale of Ragnar's Sons):, The Sagas of Ragnar Lothbrok: Norse Text, Translation, and Word List, 2nd Ed., 2021, London, Independent, 2021, p.103, ISBN 979-8475152591

It is possible that these two brothers represent Ivar and Ubba. Yngvarr is a variant spelling of Ivar, something which the composer of *Ragnarssona Þáttr* was perhaps not aware of when it was written down in the 13th century.

Husto is perhaps a variant of Ubba, and the mention of Husto's illegitimacy would agree with the account given in the *Gesta Danorum* of Ubba being born of an unnamed daughter of Esbern (*Hesbernus*) outside of his marriage with Thora Borgarhjört or Aslaug.

The *Annals of St Neots* contains a reference to the Battle of Cynwit, quoting the entry in the *Anglo-Saxon Chronicle* for the year 878. Hubba (*Ubba*), brother of Hingwar (*Ivar*) and Healfden (*Halfdan 'Hvitserk'*) invaded Devon with a naval fleet as part of the Great Heathen Army, and their three sisters wove the raven banner (*hrafnsmerki*):

Detail of a raven banner from the Bayeux tapestry.

A modern interpretation of the raven banner.

"Dicunt enim, quod tres sorores Hynguari et Hubbae, filiae videlicet Lodebrochi, illud vexillum texuerunt, et totum paraverunt illud uno meridiano tempore".
Dicunt etiam, quod in omni bello ubi praecederet idem signum, si victoriam adepturi essent, appareret in medio signi quasi corvus vivens volitans; si vero vincendi in futuro fuissent, penderet directe nihil movens.
Et hoc saepe probatum est".[47]

"They say that the three sisters of Hingwar and Hubba, daughters of Lodebroch (Lodbrok), wove that flag and got it ready in one day".

They say, moreover, that in every battle, wherever the flag went before them, if they were to gain the victory a live crow would appear flying on the middle of the flag; but if they were doomed to be defeated it would hang down motionless. And this was often proved to be so".

Legend has it that Ubba was slain in the Battle of Cynwit by Ealdorman Odda of Devon. The battle is believed to have taken place at Countisbury Hill near Countisbury in Devon.

---

[47] Asser, Stevenson, W. H. (Ed.), Vita Ælfredi regis Angul Saxonum (The Life of Alfred King of the Anglo-Saxons), 893: Together with the Annals of St Neots erroneously ascribed to Asser, 1904, Oxford, Clarendon Press, 2014, p.138
<https://archive.org/details/gri_33125000734208/page/138/mode/2up> Accessed 19/01/2022

6.   Horik I of Denmark: The Pirate King

Horik (*Hårik*) was a king of the Danes who co-ruled from around 813/814, and then became sole king from around 827/828 until his death in 854.

King Horik, 17th century engraving

Horik rose to power after a civil war with Harald 'Klak' Halfdansson and Ragnfred on one side, and Horik and his brothers on the other. In 813, when Harald and Ragnfred returned from fighting rebels in Vestfold, Norway, they were attacked by Horik and his brothers, with considerable support across the Danish realm.

Harald 'Klak' acknowledged defeat and was expelled from Denmark. He sought refuge with the new Frankish Emperor Louis the Pious, who promised to help him regain his throne.[48]. Harald was invited to share power in 819 in an attempt to achieve peace with the Franks, but was ultimately expelled from Denmark in 827.[49]

---

[48] Einhard, Dr Abel Otto (Trans.), Einhards Jahrbücher, 814:, 1888, Hannover & Leipzig, Die digitalen Monumenta Germaniae Historica (dMGH), 2004, p.129 <https://www.mgh-bibliothek.de/dokumente/b/b025198.pdf> Accessed 20/01/2022
[49] Einhard, Dr Abel Otto (Trans.), p. 160

During Horik's reign, Viking raids against the Frankish kingdoms increased dramatically, some he approved of, some he did not. Raids against Frisia were a problem.

The Franks did not have an effective fleet, so the Vikings met little in the way of effective resistance, sacking Dorestad, a centre of silver minting in 834, 835, and 836, and devastating Wacheren in 837.

In Horik's mind, successful raiders could also have presented a threat to his rule, and sometimes he punished them.

In 836 he sent an emissary to Emperor Louis declaring that he had nothing to do with the raids on Frisia, and two years later assured him that he had executed those responsible.

When the Frankish Empire broke up in 843, Horik began open hostilities towards the East and West Frankish kingdoms. In 845, a fleet under the command of one of his chiefs, Ragnar, sailed up the Seine and attacked Paris, resulting in a prize of 7,000 pounds of silver.

It is possible the same fleet attacked Hamburg on its way home, resulting in the destruction of St Mary's Cathedral, Horiks' last activity in East Francia. He assured Louis the German that he had executed some of the Viking leaders responsible.

Frisia was attacked again in 846, and the three Frankish kings agreed to unite against Horik to gain peace. Disturbances stopped around 850 when Horik began to have internal political problems.

The Viking raids in West Europe were perhaps originally a means of strengthening Horik's authority, but the Viking chiefs became increasingly harder to coordinate and were out of control.

According to the *Annales Bertiniani*, Horik and two of his nephews divided Denmark into thirds which ended the unified kingship.

> *"Oric, rex Nortmannorum, impugnantibus sese duobus nepotibus suis, bello impetitur; quibus partitione regni pacatis".[50]*
>
> "Oric, king of the Norsemen, is attacked by war with his two nephews, who attack him; with whom the partition of the kingdom was subdued".

His exiled nephew Guttorm claimed the kingdom in 854. In the following three day battle Horik was killed, along with all other rulers and a great many chiefs.

Horik II, possibly his grandson took over the throne, but disappeared some time between 864 and 873. Denmark's political stability and cohesion collapsed until king Gorm the Old reassembled the kingdom again around 936.

In the *Gesta Danorum*, Horik is referred to as "Erik" and is described as the brother of Harald Klak. Also Horik 'Barn' II (Erik the Child) is described as the son of Sigurd Snake-in-the-eye, and the grandson of Ragnar Lothbrok. This is based on the chronicle of Adam of Bremen (c1075).

---

[50] Waitz, Georg (Ed.), Annales Bertiniani (Annals of Saint Bertin), 850: MGH SS 1, 1826, Hannover & Leipzig, Die digitalen Monumenta Germaniae Historica (dMGH), 2004, p.455 <https://www.dmgh.de/mgh_ss_1/index.htm#page/445/mode/1up> Accessed 22/11/2021

# 7.	Aud the Deep-Minded (Ketilsdottir)

Aud the Deep-Minded Kettilsdottir (*Auðr djúpúðga Ketilsdóttir*) was a 9th century settler during the age of Settlement of Iceland, which is believed to have taken place between 870 and 930 (not to be confused with Aud the Deep Minded (*Ivarsdottir*) who was a legendary Norse princess who lived in the 7th or 8th century).

Aud was the second daughter of Ketill 'Flatnose' Bjornsson (*Ketill 'Flatnefr' Björnsson*), a Norwegian hersir (from the Proto-Germanic '**harisjaz*' meaning 'army's leader', a kind of local chief lord who organised and led around a hundred men with allegiance to a jarl or king).

Aud married Olaf the White (*Óláfr hinn Hvíti*), a 'sea king' who had made voyages to Britain and conquered the shire of Dublin. They had a son named Thorstein the Red (*Þorsteinn 'Rauði' Ólafsson*). Olaf was killed in battle in Ireland, and Aud and her son Thorstein travelled to the Hebrides. While there, Thorstein became a warrior king and conquered Caithness, Sutherland, Ross, Moray, and more than half of Scotland. He was later betrayed by his people and killed in battle.

Aud learned of the death of her son Thorstein while she was at Caithness. Without hope of regaining her former position, and with concern for the safety of her friends and family, Aud commissioned the construction of a knarr (*knǫrr*), a type of merchant ship built for long sea voyages. The ship was built in secret in the forest, and when it was completed, Aud captained the ship to Orkney. While there, Aud arranged the marriage of her granddaughter Groa, and then captained her ship to Breiðafjörður (broad fjord) in Iceland. *Eiríks Saga Rauða* explains:

"Auðr kom til Íslands ok var inn fyrsta vetr í Bjarnarhöfn með Birni, bróður sínum.	"Aud came to Iceland and spent the first winter in Bjarnarhofn with her brother Bjorn.
Síðan nam Auðr öll Dalalönd milli Dögurðarár ok Skraumuhlaupsár.	After that, Aud took all of the Dale land between Dogurdara and Skraumuhlapusa.
Hon bjó í Hvammi.	She settled at Hvam.
Hon hafði bænahald í Krosshólum.	She held prayers at Krossholar.
Þar lét hon reisa krossa, því at hon var skírð ok vel trúuð".[51]	There she had crosses raised, for she was baptised and a devout Christian".

As well as having twenty men under her command, Aud also had prisoners from Viking raids, who she gave their freedom once they were in Iceland. According to the social class of the time, freed slaves were no longer owned, but did not have all of the rights of a free-born man. She also gave them land to farm and make a living on.

Aud's achievements tell the story of a remarkable woman who was respected, capable, independent, and strong-willed. She was a key figure in the settlement of Iceland, and testament to the mixture of Hebridean Norse-Gael ancestry as well as that of Norwegian nobility. Her story is mentioned in *Landnámabók*, *Njáls Saga*, *Laxdæla Saga*, *Eyrbyggja Saga*, *Eiríks Saga Rauða*, and *Grettis Saga*, and is commonly credited with bringing Christianity to Iceland.

---

[51] Embleton, M. L. (Translator), Eiríks Saga Rauða (The Saga of Erik the Red):, Norse Text, Translation, and Word List, 2021, London, Independent, 2021, p.6, ISBN 979-8467805504

8.   Rorik of Dorestad: Ruler of Frisia

Rorik by Hermanus Willem Koekkoek, 1912

Rorik (*Hrœrekr*, *Hrørek*, *Rorich*) was a Danish Viking who was born around 800 and ruled over parts of Friesland between 841 and 873. He conquered Dorestad and Utrecht in 850 and swore allegiance to Louis the German in 873. He died some time between 873 and 882.

He had one brother named Harald, and it is believed that their uncle was probably Harald 'Klak' Halfdansson. It is not known for certain who his father was, since sources frequently mention the name Harald without distinction between one Harald or the other.

Harald Klak did have at least three brothers that could have been Rorik and Harald's father: Anulo (died 812), Ragnfrid (died 814), and Hemming Halfdansson (died 837).

Rorik's brother Harald had entered into an alliance with Lothair I. Lothair was involved in a conflict with his father Louis the Pious, and Frisia was part of Louis' lands. Harald's raids in Frisia were meant to weaken Louis.

When Louis died in 841, Lothair granted Harald and Rorik several parts of Friesland. His aim was to establish a military presence in Frisia with loyalty to him to protect it against his brothers and political rivals Louis the German, and Charles the Bald.

Rorik based himself at Wieringen, Harald at Walcheren. They used the islands as a base for their operations, while also ruling Dorestad. The Viking raids in Frisia decreased and were instead focused on West Francia and Anglo-Saxon England.

In 843, Lothair, Louis, and Charles signed the Treaty of Verdun, which settled their territorial disputes. Lothair no longer needed the protection of Rorik and Harald, and Lothair must have seen them as having outlived their usefulness.

In 844 they were accused of treason and imprisoned. The chronicles of the time contain doubt concerning the truthfulness of the accusation, and Rorik later managed to escape, but Harald is thought to have died in prison.

Rorik sought refuge with Louis the German and spent six years living among the Saxons before collecting a large force of Danes and embarking on raids along the northern coasts of Lothair's kingdom. In 850 he sailed into the Rhine and the Waal and seized Dorestad.

Lothair was unable to remove him without endangering his own men, and with the advice of his counsellors, Lothair realised that he was forced to accept Rorik back into fealty on the condition that he would once again handle taxes, and resist any other Viking attacks.

The *Annales Bertiniani* for that year notes:

> *"Roric nepos Herioldi,*
> *qui nuper a Lothario defecerat,*
> *assumptis Nortmannorum exercitibus,*
> *cum multitudine navium Fresiam et Batavum*
> *insulam aliaque vicina loca per Rhenum et*
> *Vahalem devastat.*
> *Quem Lotharius cum comprimere nequiret,*
> *in fidem recepit,*
> *eique Dorestadum et alios comitatus*
> *largitur".*[52]

> "Roric the nephew of Harald,
> who recently of Lothair defected,
> took his armies of the Norsemen,
> with a multitude of ships Frisia and the Dutch
> islands other near locations by the Rhine and
> the Waal devastated.
> Who Lothair with suppressing was unable,
> in faith received,
> to him he bestowed Dorestad and other
> counties".

In 873 Rorik swore allegiance to Louis the German, the *Annales Xantenses* records:

> *"Itidemque venit ad eum Ruorich,*
> *fel Christianitatis,*
> *tamen ei repositis obsidibus plurimis in navi,*
>
> *et subditus effectus est regi ac iuramentis*
> *constrictus inconcussam ei servare fidem".*[53]

> "In the same way Rorik came to him
> the gall of Christianity
> however, they replaced him with very many
> hostages in the ship,
> and became subject to the king and oaths
> to keep his faith unshaken".

There is no more mention of Rorik after 873, and it is believed that he died before 882, when Charles the Fat handed over his lands to Godfrid (*Guðfrið*), Duke of Frisia. Dorestad was in decline during this period, with changes in the course of the river systems, and merchants moving to other cities.

Rorik was perhaps one of the most powerful and influential of the Viking Danes to have been involved with the Franks. Lothair I, Lothair II, Charles the Bald, and Louis the German all accepted his long presence in Frisia, which is perhaps testament to his effectiveness as a feudal ruler, or because of a Frankish controlled decline of Dorestad.

---

[52] Waitz, Georg (Ed.), Annales Bertiniani (Annals of Saint Bertin), 850: MGH SS 1, 1826, Hannover & Leipzig, Die digitalen Monumenta Germaniae Historica (dMGH), 2004, p.455 <https://www.dmgh.de/mgh_ss_1/index.htm#page/445/mode/1up> Accessed 22/11/2021
[53] Pertz, Georg Heinrich (Ed.), Annales Xantenses (Annals of Xanten), 873: MGH SS rer. Germ. 12, 1888, Hannover & Leipzig, Die digitalen Monumenta Germaniae Historica (dMGH), 2004, p.32 <https://www.dmgh.de/mgh_ss_rer_germ_12/index.htm#page/32/mode/1up> Accessed 22/11/2021

9.   Rurik of Novgorod: The Rise of the Varangians

Rurik (*Hrøríkʀ, Рюрикъ*) was a Varangian chieftan of the Rus' people. He was invited to rule over a federation of Baltic, Finnic, and Slavic territories that would later become the Kyivan Rus' (*Garðaríki,* the 'realm of cities'). He was the founding prince of the Rurik Dynasty.

An illustration of Rurik, 1672

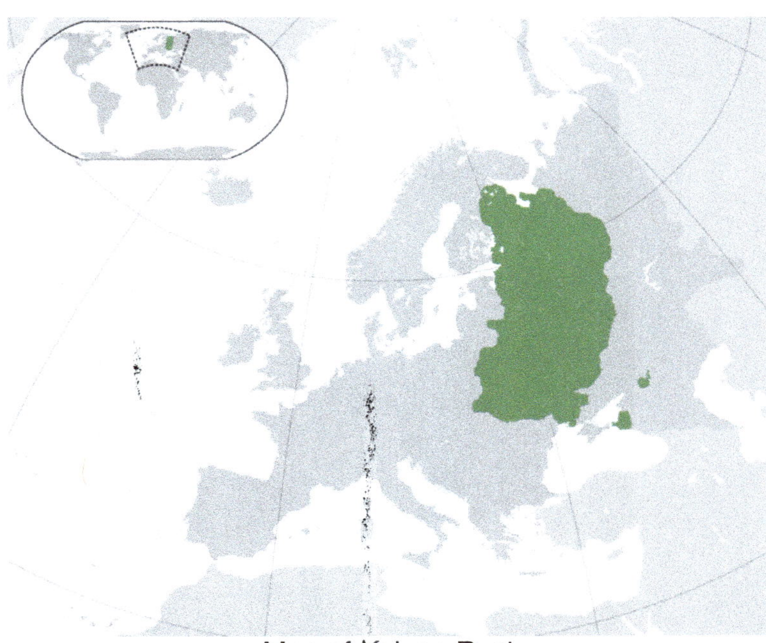

Map of Kyivan Rus'
(after the death of Yaroslav I in 1054).

Varangians were an equivalent term for Vikings in the east. In Old East Slavic speaking Eastern Europe they were called *Варяже* or *Варязи* (*Varyazhe* or *Varyazi*), and in the Greek speaking Eastern Roman Empire (Byzantium) they were called Βάραγγοι (Várangoi).

The Rus' people were Norse Scandinavians, mainly Swedes and Gotlanders, who in the 8th century began migrating east across the Baltic Sea and into Eastern Europe, across a complex system of rivers reaching to the Caspian Sea, the Black Sea, and the eastern Mediterranean. They gradually controlled strongholds, market places, and ports along the route for trading and protection against raiders. According to the Rus' Primary Chronicle, the Slavic, Baltic, and Finnic tribes refused to continue paying tribute to the Varangians and drove them out of the area, attempting to rule themselves. The tribes started fighting among themselves and decided to invite the Varangians, led by Rurik, to return and restore order in 862:

"Земля наша велика и обилна, а наряда в ней нетъ. Да поидете княжитъ и володети нами.
И изъбрашася 3 братья с роды своими, пояшапособе всю русь, и придоша: ста рейший Рюрикъ, а другий - Синеусъ на Беле-озере, а третий Изборьсте Труворъ.

"Our land is great and plentiful, but there is no order in it. Come reign and rule over us.
And three brothers with their clans were elected and took all of Russia with them, and they came to the Slavs, and the elder Rurik came, and the other - Sineus - sat on Beloozero, and the third - Truvor - in Izborsk.

От техъ прозвася Руская земля, новугородьци, ти суть людье ноугородьциот рода варяжьска. Преже бо беша словени.

And from those Varangians the Russian land was nicknamed. Novgorodians are those people from the Varangian family, and before that they were Slavs.

По двуже лету Синеусъ умре и братъ его Труворъ.

Two years later, Sineus and his brother Truvor died.

И прия власть Рюрикъ, и раздая мужемъ своимъ грады: о вому Полотескъ, о вому Ростовъ, д ругому Белоозеро". [54]

And one Rurik seized all the power, and began to distribute cities to his men - Polotsk to that, Rostov to that, Beloozero to another".

The Arrival of Rurik to Ladoga by Viktor Vasnetsov (1848-1926)

The Rus' used the Volga trade route to trade with Muslim countries on the south shores of the Caspian Sea, sometimes as far inland as Baghdad, trading in furs, weapons, and Christian slaves. Silver dirham coins have been found in treasure hoards as far west as Dublin.

Rurik remained in power until his death in 879, and the Keivan Rus' lasted until the Mongol invasion of 1236-1242. The Rurik Dynasty ultimately ruled the Tsardom of Russia until 1598, and numerous noble Rusian and Ruthenian families claim descent from Rurik.

The last Rurikid to rule Russia was Tsar Vasily IV from the House of Shuysky, cadet branch of the House of Ruril, who reigned until 1612.

---

[54] The Russian Primary Chronicles (Povest' Vremennykh Let, Повѣсть времаньныхъ лѣтъ):
Laurentian Codex, F.p.IV.2, 1377, St. Petersburg, National Library of Russia, 2012, л.7
<http://expositions.nlr.ru/LaurentianCodex/_Project/page_Show.php?lang=en> Accessed 12/02/2022

10.   Guthrum 'Æthelstan': The Danelaw

Guthrum (*Guðrum*) was a Danish Viking, one of the leaders of the Great Summer Army, and King of East Anglia between 879 and around 890. In 871 the Great Summer Army arrived in Reading to join forces with the Great Heathen Army and conquer all of the Anglo-Saxon kingdoms. The combined forces were successful in conquering the kingdoms of East Anglia, Mercia, and Northumbria, and by 878 they had overrun Wessex.

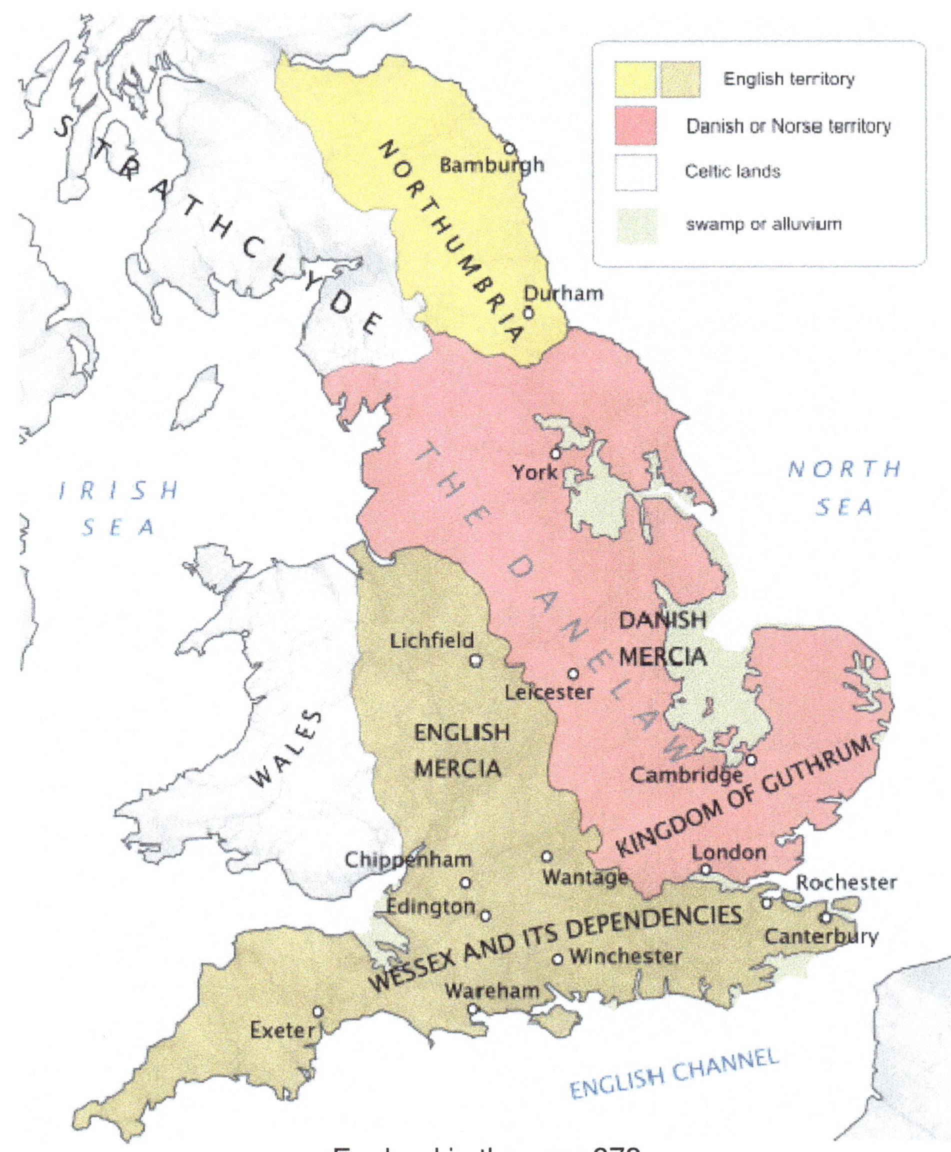

England in the year 878

Between the 6th and 12th May 878, Guthrum's forces met the West Saxons led by Alfred the Great at the Battle of Edington.

The West Saxons decisively defeated the Danes, who retreated to their stronghold where Alfred laid siege, and eventually Guthrum surrendered.

Under the terms of the surrender, Guthrum was baptised as a Christian with the name Æthelstan ('noble stone') and then left Wessex and Mercia and returned to East Anglia, with an agreement on the legitimacy and boundaries of their territories, and provisions for lasting peace terms.

The treaty between Alfred and Æthelstan was the foundation for what became known as the Danelaw, the part of England where the laws of the Danes were in effect.

The area of the Danelaw roughly corresponds with 15 shires: Bedford, Buckingham, Cambridge, Derby, Essex, Hertford, Huntingdon, Leicester, Lincoln, Middlesex, Norfolk, Northampton, Nottingham, Suffolk, and York. Scandinavian York or Danish York (*Jórvík*) became a powerful economic centre and minted its own coins.

Anglo-Saxons living side by side with Scandinavians brought about a change in the Old English language, which was influenced by Old Norse, resulting in a simplification of grammar, and Anglo-Norse dialects, even after the Danelaw was annexed by the Anglo-Saxons in 954.

11.   Gardar Svavarsson: Finding Iceland

Gardar Svavarsson (*Garðar Svavarsson*) was a Swedish Viking who according to the sagas, briefly lived in Iceland. He was the second Scandinavian to reach Iceland after Naddod (*Naddoðr*), and the first to circumnavigate Iceland. He owned some land in Zealand in modern day Denmark, and was married to a woman from *Suðreyjar* (the 'Southern Islands' or 'the Hebrides').

One of the reasons given for Gardar's arrival at Iceland was that he had attempted to sail to *Suðreyjar* to claim his inheritance from his father-in-law, and after sailing into a storm at Pentland Firth, the strait between the Ornkeys and Caithness, the storm pushed his ship far north until he reached what was later referred to as the 'Eastern Horn', meaning the mountains on the east coast of Iceland.

Another reason given is that Gardar had heard of Naddod's discovery of a new land called *Snæland* ('snow land'), and his mother, who was a seeress, advised him on going there. Either way, when he arrived at Iceland he explored the coastline until he had successfully circumnavigated the land, confirming that it was indeed an island.

While sailing along the north coast he went ashore in an area later known as *Skjálfandi*, which literally means shaking or trembling, perhaps in reference to earthquakes in the area.

In around 870, he built himself a house and spent the winter there, and the place was then called *Húsavík* ('house bay' or 'bay of houses'), the first place in Iceland to be settled by a Norseman.

The following spring when Gardar set sail, a boat drifted away from him with a man called Nattfari (*Náttfari*) aboard, with a slave and a bondwoman.

Nattfari settled at a place that was since called Nattfaravik, but the *Landnámabók* tells us that this was not a permanent settlement.

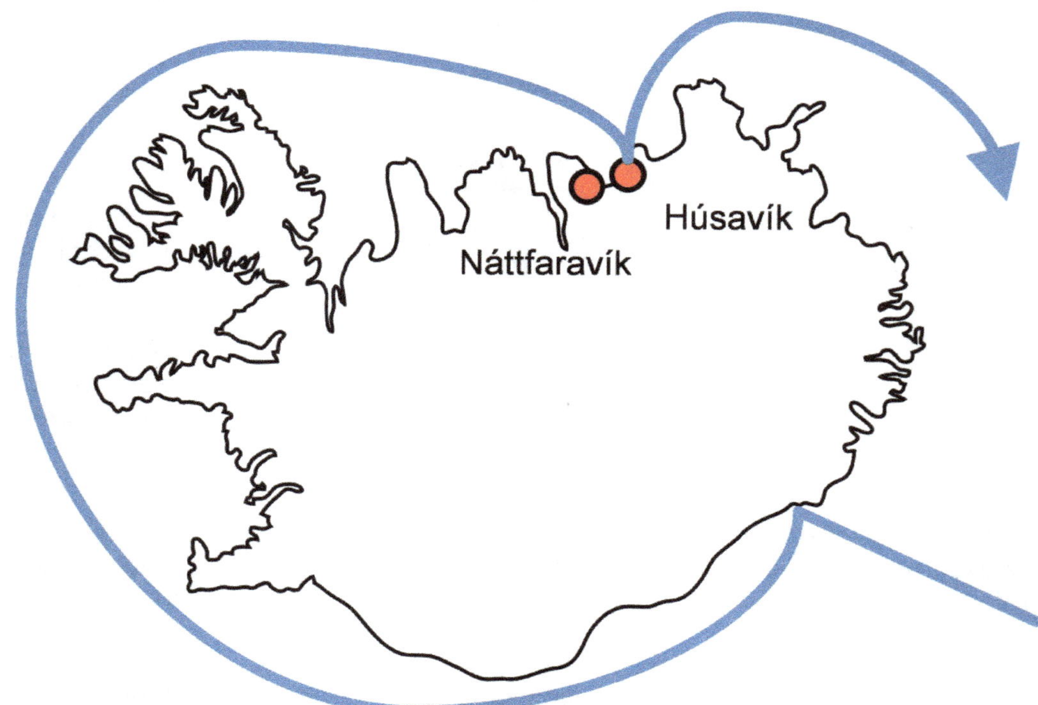

Gardar's journey around Iceland, Image by the Author

Gardar returned to Norway full of praise of the new land and named it *Garðarshólmi* (Gardar's islet). It is not known what happened to him afterwards.

His son *Uni Danski* (Uni the Dane) emigrated to Iceland and tried to claim it for the Norwegian king with himself as earl. When the local farmers found out about his intentions, they would not help him in any way, and he was soon killed.

The principal source of information for Gardar is the *Landnámabók* (the 'Book of Land Taking' or the 'Book of Settlements'):

"Maður hét Garðar Svavarsson, sænskur að ætt; *hann fór að leita Snælands að tilvísan móður sinnar framsýnnar.*	"A man was named Gardar Svavarsson, Swedish by descent; he travelled to seek Snæland at the advice of his mother who was foresighted.
Hann kom að landi fyrir austan Horn hið eystra; þar var þá höfn.	He came to land east before the east of the eastern horn, there was then a harbour.
Garðar sigldi umhverfis landið og vissi, að það var eyland. *Hann var um veturinn norður í Húsavík á Skjálfanda og gerði þar hús.* *Um vorið, er hann var búinn til hafs, sleit frá honum mann á báti, er hét Náttfari, og þræl og ambátt.*	Garðar sailed around the land and knew it was an island. He was about winter north in Húsavík in Skjálfandi and made there a house. About spring, when he was preparing to the sea, broke from him a man in a boat, who was named Náttfari and a slave and a handmaid.
Hann byggði þar síðan, er heitir Náttfaravík. *Garðar fór þá til Noregs og lofaði mjög landið.* *Hann var faðir Una, föður Hróars Tungugoða.* *Eftir það var landið kallað Garðarshólmur, og var þá skógur milli fjalls og fjöru".*[55]	He settled there since, and it was called Náttfaravík. Gardar travelled then to Norway and praised much the land. He was the father of Una, the father of Hróar Tungugoði. After that was the land called Garðarshólmur, and was there forest between the mountain and the shore".

Uni Danski had a son called *Hróar Tungugoði* who inherited the estate, but quarrelled with others and was twice challenged to a hill battle, winning both times.

He was eventually murdered, and the murder was avenged by his son. This was indicative of the many feuds and cycles of revenge killings that plagued Iceland in its early history.

Hroar's wife was Arngunnur, the sister of Gunnar Hamnudarson, who was one of the main characters in Njal's Saga, the longest and perhaps the greatest of the Icelandic Sagas.

---

[55] Sturla Þórðarson (Ed.) & Eiríkur Rögnvaldsson (Ed.), Landnámabók: Sturlubók, 13th Century, Iceland, Netútgáfan (Online Version), 1998, <https://www.snerpa.is/net/snorri/landnama.htm> Accessed 21/01/2022

12.   Hastein: Scourge of the Mediterranean

Viking Leader Hasting (Hastein) at Luni, Italy
Histoire Populaire de la France, 1862

Hastein (*Hásteinn*) was a Danish Viking chieftan who took part in raids around the Frankish Empire, the Iberian Peninsula, and in the Mediterranean along with Bjorn 'Ironside', one of the sons of Ragnar Lothbrok.

The Danish Vikings were well aware of the political situation in the Frankish Empire and the conflicts between the descendants of the Frankish Emperor Charlemagne.

They took advantage of the Frankish civil wars by raiding where defences were weak, occupying strategic places along the Loire and the Seine, and forming alliances with the different kings who sought to benefit from their activities by weakening the kingdoms of their rivals.

Some of the biggest raids occurred at Antwerp and Noirmoutier in 836, Rouen in 841, Quentovic and Nantes in 842, and Paris in 845.

In Scandinavia the rival chieftains and kings saw Viking raids as a means of gaining wealth, which would ultimately strengthen their position against their rivals, who they were in constant competition with.

The Mediterranean coast must have presented itself as an interesting new prospect, as the soft underbelly of Europe, and in 859, Hastein and Bjorn set off from the Loire with a fleet of 62 ships and headed south towards the north coast of the Iberian Peninsula.

The state of Asturias in north Western Spain was aware of the Vikings and their activities to the north, having heard from their Frankish contacts. They were already well prepared to fend off attacks from the rest of Iberia which was under Muslim rule at the time. Such preparation meant that they were able to fend off the Viking attacks, and the Muslim ruled Umayyad Caliphate of Cordoba was also able to fend them off at Niebla.

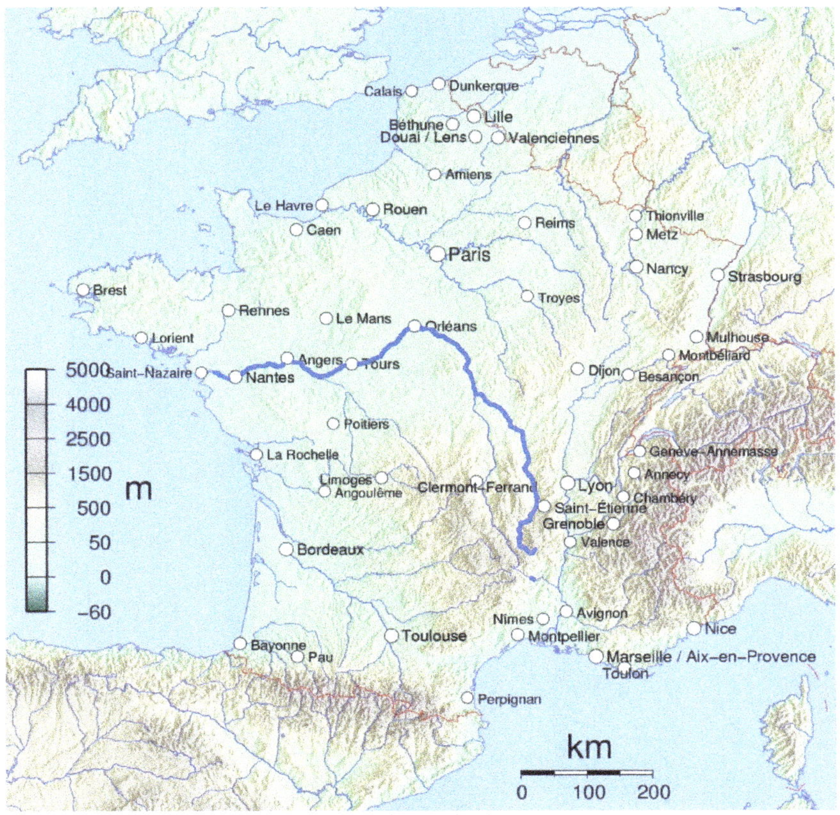

The River Loire

The River Seine and surrounding basin

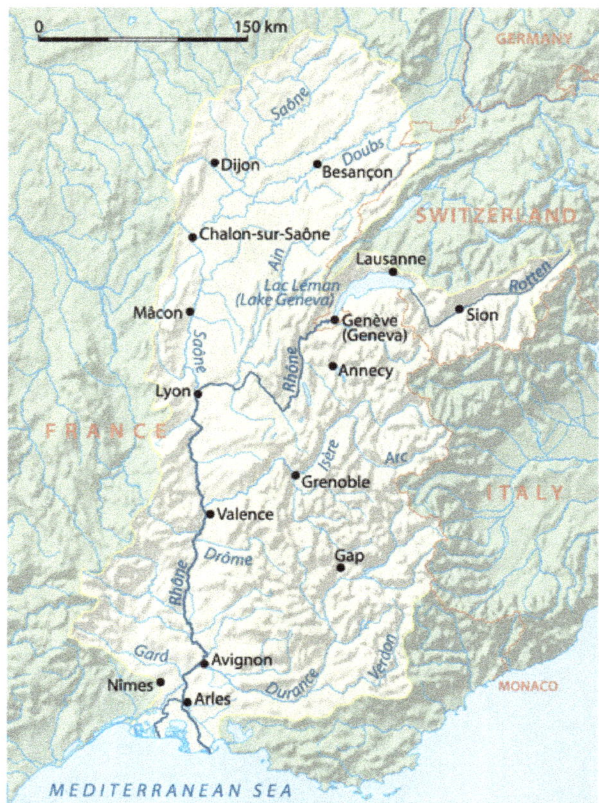

The River Rhone from Geneva south to the Mediterranean

Despite these early defeats, Hastein and Bjorn continued through the Straight of Gibraltar, where they met less resistance, sacking the town of Algeciras and burning down its mosque, and then crossing over to the Idrisid Caliphate on the North African coast and ravaging the city of Mazimma (*al-Husaima* or *Al Hoceima*), and occupying Nekor (*Nekkour*) for 8 days.

Heading along the southern coast of Spain, they raided the city of Orihuela, and then attacked the Balearic Islands before heading north to follow the south coast of Francia. They camped at the island of Camargue at the mouth of the Rhone for the winter, and then attacked Narbonne, Nîmes, Arles, and struck further inland at Valence and Roussillon.

Perhaps having heard stories of a famous ancient city that had once been part of the Roman Empire four centuries earlier, Rome had always been the ultimate destination for their voyage. Conquering such a famous city would have earned legendary status for those who were bold enough to achieve it. The city they actually conquered was in fact Luni, some 200 miles north of their target, a fact they apparently learned only afterwards.

For the attack at Luni, Hastein undertook a particularly cunning plan reminiscent of the Trojan Horse. He had his men carry him to the city gates, where he told the guards that he was dying and that he wished to convert to Christianity and receive last rites.

In an act of Christian kindness his wish was granted, and a small group of men were allowed through the gates to carry Hastein on a stretcher to the city church, where he received the sacraments. He then jumped up from his stretcher, and led his men to fight their way to the town gates to allow the rest of their forces to enter the gates and sack the city.

Another account tells us that after Hastein had made his request for last rites at the city gates, he then feigned his death the next day, being carried into the city in a coffin rather than a stretcher with 50 men concealing swords under their robes. During or after the service, he leapt out from inside the coffin, decapitated the priest, and then sacked the city. The validity of this account has been much debated.

After attacking Luna, Hastein and his forces continued down the west coast of Italy sacking the city of Pisa, and then sailing up the river Arno to raid the town of Fiesole. It is also thought that they could have possibly continued on to territories of the Byzantine Empire in the eastern Mediterranean.

On their return journey through the Strait of Gibraltar, a Muslim fleet was waiting for them. Perhaps this fleet had been formed to catch these Vikings and exact revenge upon them for the attacks on their land.

The Strait of Gibraltar was like a bottle neck, a great place for an ambush, and since it had been blocked by the Muslim fleet, the Vikings had little option but to fight their way through.

Some accounts say that the Vikings lost 40 ships in this encounter, while some say that they merely lost two ships, but lost 40 in a storm.

Either way, they went on to attack Pamplona in the Kingdom of Navarre before returning home to the Loire with 20 ships in 862.

Hastein then settled in Brittany, where he allied himself with Salomon, the King of Brittany, and on the 2nd July 866, a joint Breton-Danish army fought against the Franks at the Battle of Brissarthe.

The Breton-Danish army set off on an expedition into Anjou, Maine, and Touraine, sacking Le Mans in the process.

Robert the Strong assembled an army to expel the Danes, joined by Ranulf of Poitou, Gauzfrid, and Hérve of Maine. They intercepted the Danes before they reached their boats on the river Loire and in the ensuing battle Hastein killed Robert the Strong, Ranulf was killed by an arrow, and the Franks retreated.

Hastein remained in the Loire country until he was expelled by Charles the Bald in 882. He relocated his army north to the Seine, and when Paris was besieged by the Franks, he turned his attention towards England.

By this time Hastein would have been a seasoned and experienced Viking whose deeds would have been well known to many.

After a confrontation with Alfred the Great between Milton Regis and Appledore in Kent, Hastein came to terms with Alfred and allowed his two sons to be baptised. He left Kent and relocated to a fortified camp at Benfeet in Essex.

He launched further raids on Mercia and received reinforcements from the settled Danes of East Anglia and York, moving to Chester.

After many strikes and counter-strikes, Hastein's forces were chased across the midlands, before dispersing into East Anglia, and those who were left found passage back to the Seine. There are no further accounts of Hastein after 896.

13.   Raven-Floki Vilgerdarsson: Finding Iceland

Raven-Floki Vilgerdarsson (*Hrafna-Flóki Vilgerðarson*) was the first Norseman to intentionally sail to Iceland. It had originally been discovered by Naddodd (*Naddoðr*) and called Snowland (*Snæland*). It was then circumnavigated by Gardar Svavarsson (*Garðar Svavarsson*) and called Gardar's Islet (*Garðarshólmi*). Floki's story is documented in Chapter 2 of the *Landnámabók*, an account of the settlement or 'land taking' (*landnám*) of Iceland by the Norse people in the 9th and 10th centuries.

A page of the *Landnámabók*

The exact year of Floki's arrival in Iceland is unclear, but it is believed that he set off from Western Norway in 868 with his wife Gró, his children Oddleif (*Oddleifr*) and Thjodgerd (*Þjóðgerður*).

Also travelling with them were three men named Thorolf (*Þórólfr*), Herjolf (*Herjólfr*) and Faxe (*Faxi*).

They stopped at the Shetland Islands and the Faroe Islands, and from there Raven-Floki took three ravens with him, earning the nickname Raven-Floki (*Hrafna-Flóki*).

"Flóki hafði hrafna þrjá með sér í haf,	"Flóki had three ravens with him in the sea,
og er hann lét lausan hinn fyrsta, fló sá aftur um stafn;	and when he released the first one, it was seen to fly after the stem of the ship;
annar fló í loft upp og aftur til skips;	another flew in the air up and back to the ship;
hinn þriðji fló fram um stafn í þá átt,	the third flew forward about the stem of the ship in the direction,
sem þeir fundu landið.	in which they found the land.
Þeir komu austan að Horni og sigldu fyrir sunnan landið".[56]	They came east to the Horn and sailed for the south of the country".

They sailed west past Reykjanes and saw a large bay. Faxe said that they seemed to have found a great land. The bay facing Reykjavik was from then on known as Faxe's Bay (*Faxaflói*). Flóki set up a winter camp in Vatnsfjörður at Barðaströnd. The weather during the summer was deceptively fair, and they were not prepared for the coldness of the winter that followed. While waiting for the spring to come and the weather to improve, Floki hiked up the highest mountain above his camp and spotted a large fjord which was full of drifting ice (*Ísafjörður*). After this he named the island Iceland (*Ísland*).

---

[56] Sturla Þórðarson (Ed.) & Eiríkur Rögnvaldsson (Ed.), Landnámabók: Sturlubók, 13th Century, Iceland, Netútgáfan (Online Version), 1998, <https://www.snerpa.is/net/snorri/landnama.htm> Accessed 21/01/2022

"Þeir Flóki sigldu vestur yfir Breiðafjörð og tóku þar land, sem heitir Vatnsfjörður við Barðaströnd.

Þá var fjörðurinn fullur af veiðiskap, og gáðu þeir eigi fyrir veiðum að fá heyjanna, og dó allt kvikfé þeirra um veturinn.

Vor var heldur kalt.

Þá gekk Flóki upp á fjall eitt hátt og sá norður yfir fjöllin fjörð fullan af hafísum; því kölluðu þeir landið Ísland, sem það hefir síðan heitið".[57]

"Flóki and his men sailed west over Breiðafjörður and landed there, which is called Vatnsfjörður by Barðaströnd.

Then the fjord was full of fishing, and they could not afford to catch the hay, and all their livestock died during the winter.

Spring was rather cold.

Then Flóki went up the mountain one way and saw north over the mountains a fjord full of sea ice; therefore they called the land Iceland, which it has since been called".

Hrafna-Floki's journey, Image by the author

When they later returned to Norway there was great discussion about the new land that had been found. Floki believed that the land was worthless, while Herjolf believed that the land had good and bad qualities, and Thorolf claimed that butter was smeared on every straw on the land that they had found, and he was then nicknamed Thorolf Butter (*Þórólfur Smjör*). Although Floki believed that the island of Iceland was worthless, he later returned and settled there until his death.

---

[57] Sturla Þórðarson (Ed.) & Eiríkur Rögnvaldsson (Ed.), Landnámabók: Sturlubók, 13th Century, Iceland, Netútgáfan (Online Version), 1998, <https://www.snerpa.is/net/snorri/landnama.htm> Accessed 21/01/2022

14.   Rollo of Normandy: The First Normans

Rollo, Duke of Normandy, 13th century

Rollo (*Rolf, Hrólfr, Gǫngu-Hrólfr, Rou, Rollon, Rolloun*) was a Viking who raided in Scotland, Ireland, and West Francia, becoming the first ruler of Normandy in northern France. He was apparently known as '*Gǫngu-Hrólfr*' (Rolf-the-Walker), *Haralds Saga Hárfagra* explains:

"Hrólfr var vikingr mikill;	"Hrolf was a Viking great;
hann var svá mikill maðr vexti,	he was so much a man grown,
at engi hestr mátti bera hann,	that no horse may bear him,
ok gekk hann,	and he walked,
hvargi sem hann fór;	wherever that he travelled;
hann var kallaðr Gǫngu-Hrólfr".[58]	he was called Rolf-the-Walker".

Orkneyinga Saga also mentions his nickname and his father's connection to King Harald Fairhair:

"Rögnvaldr jarl gekk til lands með	"Rognvald earl seized lands with
Haraldi hinum hárfagra,	Harald the Fairhair,
en hann gaf honum yfirsókn um Mæri	but he gave him lordship about Maeren
hváratveggju ok Raumsdal;	and Romsdale;
hann átti Ragnhildi dóttur Hrólfs nefju;	he married Ragnhild, the daughter of Hrolf the Nosy;
þeirra sonr var Hrólfr er vann Norðmandi,	their son was Hrolf who won Normandy,
hann var svá mikill, at hann báru eigi hestar,"	he was so great, that he was borne by no horse,"
því hèt hann Göngu-Hrólfr;	for that he was named Rolf-the-Walker;
frá honum eru komnir Rúðu-jarlar ok Engla-konúngar,[59]	from him came the Rouen earls and English kings;

---

[58] Snorri Sturluson, Heimskringla: Haralds Saga Hárfagra, c1220s, Iceland, Heimskringla.no, 2020, <https://heimskringla.no/wiki/Haraldz_saga_ins_hárfagra_(FJ)> Accessed 13/02/2022

Viking raids up the Seine began in 820, and by 911 the area had been raided many times. There were even small Viking settlements in the lower Seine area used as bases to launch attacks further up river or inland.

The town of Chartres had been attacked and burned in 858, and it had since been rebuilt and strengthened. Rollo had made a reputation for himself as an outstanding warrior, and In 911 he led a force of Danish Vikings to lay Siege to Chartres once more.

According to legend, Bishop Gantelme displayed the tunic of the Virgin Mary on the ramparts and led a charge of peasants against the Vikings who fled.

The Frankish cavalry then pursued them, and not having enough time to escape, the Vikings built a defensive wall by slaughtering the livestock from their ships.

The cavalry halted as the horses were intimidated by the sight and smell of the livestock corpses. The Franks were unable to attack, and they instead opened negotiations with Rollo, who was able to persuade Charles III of West Francia (also known as 'Charles the Simple' or 'Charles the Straightforward') that they might instead become valuable allies.

The battle was ended, and both sides formulated the Treaty of Saint-Clair-sur-Epte. Charles granted Rollo lands between the mouth of the Seine and Rouen which were originally part of Neustria.

In return Rollo agreed to end his raiding, swear allegiance to Charles, convert to Christianity, and defend the estuary of the Seine from other Viking raiders.

The territory that Rollo was given dukedom over was called 'Normandy', meaning 'the place of the Northmen'. The term 'Northman' is clearly composed of the words 'north' and 'man' in Germanic languages such as Old Norse and Anglo-Saxon.

It was borrowed into other languages (e.g. Gallicised into Old French, Latinised into Latin, etc.) resulting in a number of different spellings:

	Northman	Northmen		Normandy
Proto-Germanic	*Nurþrą-*mann	*Nurþrą-*manniz		
Old Norse	Norðmaðr	Norðmenn	=	Norðmanndi
Anglo-Saxon	Norþmann	Norþmenn	=	Normandiġ
Old French	Normant	Normanz	=	Normendie
Latin	Nortmannus	Nortmannæ	=	Nortmannia
	Normannus	Normannæ	=	Normannia
	Nordmannus	Nordmannæ	=	Nordmannia

First recorded as the leader of the settlers in a charter of 918, Rollo continued to reign over the region until at least 928.

---

[59] Orkneyinga Saga, Orkneyinga Saga: History of the Earls of Orkney, 13th Century, Iceland, Heimskringla.no, 2019, <https://heimskringla.no/wiki/Orkneyinga_saga> Accessed 14/02/2022

Rollo and his descendants assimilated and intermingled with the West Franks and Gallo-Roman peoples, learning and adopting the language of Old Frankish and Gallo-Romance '*Langues d'oïl*'.

They also brought many Norse loan words into the mix that would later become known as the 'Old Norman' and 'Anglo-Norman' branches of 'Old French'.

Norse settlement in the Duchy of Normandy was mostly around the coast and the capital of Rouen, this gradually spread west to include Caen and Cherbourg, and by 1050 was roughly equivalent to the region of Normandy today.

The Channel Islands were granted to Rollo's son and successor William I Londsword in 933 by King Raoul of Western Francia, which resulted in the dialects of Old Norman which became known as *Jèrriais* (Jersey French) and *Guernésiais* (Guernsey French).

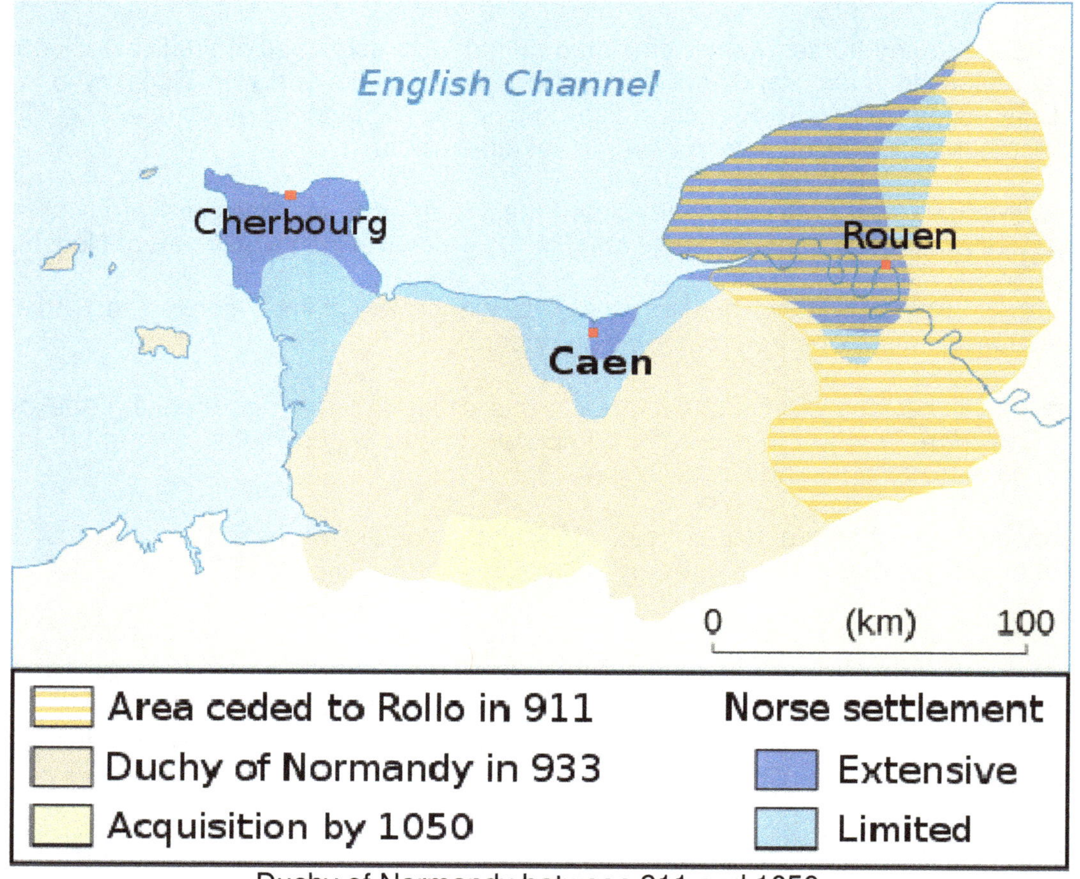

Duchy of Normandy between 911 and 1050

The Normans went on to conquer England under William the Conqueror (Rollo's great-great-great grandson), and play an active part in the Crusades.

15.   Ingolf Arnarsson: Settling Iceland

Igolf takes over Iceland, by Johan Peter Raadsig, 1850

Ingolf Arnarsson (*Ingólfr Arnarson, Ingolfr Landnamsmaðr*) was born around 849 in the village of Sunnfjord in western Norway.

He became the first permanent Norse settler of Iceland, exploring the island from 867 to 870, and founding the settlement of Reykjavik ('smoky bay' or 'steamy bay') in around 874. Archaeologists believe that the settlement of Iceland may have begun earlier, and Chapter 1 of the *Íslendingabók* mentions that there were Irish monks living on Iceland first:

"Í þann tíð var Ísland viði vaxit á milli fjalls ok fjöru.

"In that time was Iceland wooded grown between the mountains and the shore.

Þá váru hér menn kristnir, þeir er Norðmenn kalla Papa, en þeir fóru síðan á braut,
af því at þeir vildu eigi vera hér við heiðna menn, ok létu eftir bækr írskar ok bjöllur ok bagla.

There were here men who were Christians, they who the Northmen call Papar, but they travelled since away, because they did not want to be alongside heathen people, and left they after behind Irish books, bells and croziers.

Af því mátti skilja, at þeir váru menn írskir".

Of which therefore it may be known, that they were men who were Irish".[60]

---

[60] Ari Þorgilsson, Íslendingabók:, 12th century, Iceland, Heimskringla.no, 2013, <http://www.heimskringla.no/wiki/%C3%8Dslendingab%C3%B3k> Accessed 14/02/2022

Chapter 6 of the *Landnámabók* mentions Ingolf's arrival at Iceland:

> *"Þá er Ingólfur sá Ísland,*
> *skaut hann fyrir borð öndugissúlum sínum til heilla;*
> *hann mælti svo fyrir, að hann skyldi þar byggja,*
> *er súlurnar kæmi á land".*

> "When Ingolf saw Iceland,
> he launched over board his high-seat-pillars as an omen;
> he said then so, that he should there dwell,
> where the pillars came to land".[61]

His two slaves Karl and Vífil searched the coastline for three years before finally finding the pillars in a small bay which eventually became Reykjavik.

Meanwhile Ingolf's step-brother Hjorleif had been murdered by his Irish slaves, and Ingolf hunted them down and killed them in the area later called Vestmannaeyjar ('west man islands'), *vestmenn* ('west men') is a term that Norse people used for Irishmen.

Chapter 2 of *Grœnlendinga Saga* mentions Ingolf *landnamsmaðr* ('land-taking-man') as a kinsman of Herjolf Bardarson. Ingolf gave Herjolf land in Iceland:

> *"Herjólfr var Bárðarson Herjólfssonar.*
>
> *Hann var frændi Ingólfs landnámamanns.*
> *Þeim Herjólfi gaf Ingólfr land á milli Vágs ok Reykjaness.*
> *Herjólfr bjó fyrst á Drepstokki.*
> *Þorgerðr hét kona hans, en Bjarni sonr þeira ok var inn efniligsti maðr".*[62]

> "Herjolf was Bard's son, the son of Herjolf.
>
> He was kinsman to Ingolf the land taking man.
> Ingolf gave to them land between Vogs and Reykjanes.
> Herjolf lived first at Drepstokk.
> His wife was named Thorgerd and their son Bjarni was a promising man".

Ingolf oversaw matters of administration as a kind of priest or chieftain, an important role which would come to be known as a '*Goði*' or '*Goðorðsmaðr*'. The area under his control and influence would come to be called a '*Goðorð*'.

Ingolf married Hallveig Fróðadóttir, and their son was Thorstein Ingolfson (*Þorsteinn Ingólfsson*).

Thorstein inherited the title of Goði and was a powerful a chieftain who founded the first assembly, laying the foundation for the later parliament known as the Althingi (*Alþingi*).

---

[61] Sturla Þórðarson (Ed.) & Eiríkur Rögnvaldsson (Ed.), Landnámabók: Sturlubók, 13th Century, Iceland, Netútgáfan (Online Version), 1998, <https://www.snerpa.is/net/snorri/landnama.htm> Accessed 21/01/2022

[62] Embleton, M. L. (Translator), Grœnlendinga Saga (The Saga of the Greenlanders):, Norse Text, Translation, and Word List, 13th Century, London, Independent, 2021, p.8, ISBN 979-8464540590

16.   Harald 'Fairhair': King of all Norway

Harald Fairhair, from the Flateyjarbók, 14th century, Iceland

Harald Fairhair (*Haraldr Hálfdanarson, Haraldr Lufa, Haraldr inn Hárfagri*) is a legendary king of Norway, and the first king to rule all of Norway. He is believed to have reigned from around 872 to 930.

Much of what we know about Harald comes from the Sagas written around three centuries after his lifetime. Many accounts differ on many points, but one thing that is agreed upon is that Harald had unified Norway into one kingdom.

Haralds Saga Hárfagra tells us that part of Harald's ambition to rule over all of Norway was brought about as a result of a marriage proposal to a woman named Gyda, daughter of King Eirik of Hordaland. She received the proposal from Harald's envoys and answered that she refused to marry Harald before he was king over all Norway.

"Þá mælti Gyða við sendimenn,
bað þá bera þau orð sín Haraldi konungi,
at hon mun því at einu játa at gerask eigin kona hans,
ef hann vill þat gera fyrir hennar sakir áðr,
at leggja undir sik allan Nóreg
ok ráða því ríki jafnfrjálsliga,

sem Eiríkr konungr Svía-veldi eða Gormr konungr Danmǫrku,

"Then spoke Gyði with the envoys,
and bade them bare their words to Harald the King,
that she would therefore at once confess to make herself his only wife,
if he wished to do so for her sake after,

to subdue under him all Norway,
and rule therefore the kingdom equally freely,

as Erik the king of Sweden or Gormr the king of Denmark,

þvíat þá þykki mér, segir hon,
hann mega heita þjóðkonungr".[63]

because so seems to me, said she, he may be called the king of the nation".

He vowed not to cut his hair until he had attained his goal, and as his hair grew he was referred to as '*Haraldr Lufa*' ('lufa' meaning 'thick hair', 'matted hair', or 'scruffy hair'). After he had completed his conquests and subdued his remaining enemies, he had his hair cut and was then called '*hárfagri*' (meaning 'beautiful hair' or 'handsome hair').

In the year 866, Harald began a series of conquests over the minor kingdoms that made up all of Norway, beginning with the Upplands and Trondheim. His success is believed to be due to his excellent leadership skills, military reforms, and the help and advice of his uncle Guthorm.

The taxes that Harald demanded from his subjects were much higher than other kings, and a third of all revenues were given to his jarls. This made jarls and rich farmers loyal to him in order to benefit from this increase.

All lands and lakes were declared the property of the king, and all land owners became tenants of the king's land which they had previously owned, and they subsequently owed him a duty. Many people saw this large increase in tax as tyrannical, and the people who were most affected by these reforms left Norway for Iceland, Scotland, Orkney, Shetland, the Hebrides, and the Faroe Islands.

Around the year 872, the Battle of Hafrsfjord was fought in Rogaland in Western Norway. Erik of Hordaland and Kjotve the Rich of Agder attacked Harald and were defeated. Large numbers of Harald's opponents then fled to the same places as those who had sought to escape Harald's tyranny.

Harald was forced to make an expedition to the West to clear the islands and the Scottish mainland of any chieftains or jarls hiding there, so as to prevent any uprisings, rebellions, or attacks on the profitable shipment of goods that had now been brought under tight control.

Some say that this expedition never happened, and that it was added to the narrative of the Sagas as a reflection of the anxieties felt at the time, when Norway had begun to increase its dominance over Iceland.

Harald's later reign was made difficult by the conflicts between his sons, which threatened the stability of his rule. The number of sons varies by account to somewhere between 11 and 20. His favourite son however was Erik Bloodaxe who co-ruled with him when he reached 80 years old. Their co-rule lasted for three years until Harald died around the year 933. After which there began a period of conflict and struggle between Harald's many sons from different wives over inherited lands and control which destabilised Norway.

Harald became an important icon of Norwegian nationalism in the 19th century during Norway's struggle for independence from Sweden. He is something of a national hero, seen by many as the father of the Norwegian nation. He is also arguably an indirect or inadvertent father of the Icelandic nation, since it was during his rule, and as a result of his rule, that so many people left Norway and settled in Iceland. In this light it is perhaps possible to see Harald Fairhair as both a tyrant and a hero, depending on one's point of view.

---

[63] Snorri Sturluson, Heimskringla: The Saga of Harald Fairhair (Haralds Saga Hárfagra), c1220s, Iceland, Heimskringla.no, 2020, <https://heimskringla.no/wiki/Haraldz_saga_ins_h%C3%A1rfagra_(FJ)> Accessed 17/02/2022

17.   Erik Bloodaxe: The Brother-Slayer

Erik Bloodaxe (*Eirikr Haraldsson, Eirikr Blóðöxi, Eirik Fratrum Interfector*) was a 10th century Norwegian king. He was the son of Harald I 'Fairhair'. He had co-ruled with his father Harald from 930 to 933, and Harald had intended Erik to succeed him on the throne. The nickname 'Bloodaxe' (*Blóðöxi*) was given to Erik because he killed four of his half-brothers in order to hold on to the crown of Norway. He was also given the Latin nickname '*fratrum interfector*' (literally 'brother-killer', 'brother-bane' or 'brother-slayer').

Haralds Saga Hárfagra tells us that Erik was the favourite son of Harald, and that he distinguished himself as a Viking warrior from an early age:

"Þá er Eiríkr var 12 vetra gamall, gaf Haraldr konungr honum fim langskip, ok fór hann í hernaði, fyrst í Austrveg ok þá suðr um Danmörk ok um Frísland ok Saxland,

ok dvaldist í þeirri ferð 4 vetr.
…
Eptir þat fór hann norðr á Finnmörk ok alt til Bjarmalands, ok átti hann þar orrostu mikla ok hafði sigr".[64]

"Then when Erik was 12 winters old, gave King Harald to him five longships, and travelled he raiding, first in the eastern way (Baltic), and then south about Denmark and Friesland and Saxland (Saxony), and dwelt he on this voyage 4 winters.
…
After that travelled he north to Finnmark and all the way to Bjarmaland, and had he there battles great and had victory".

Erik is also also thought to be the same person as 'Erik of Northumbria' or 'Erik of York' who ruled in Northumbria from 947 to 948, and again from 952 to 954. This has however been called into question and challenged by modern scholars.

One of Erik's half-brothers was Haakon, known as Hákon 'the Good' (*Hákon Góði*), or Haakon 'the foster of Æthelstan' (*Hákon Aðalsteinsfóstri*). He had been fostered and converted to Christianity by Æthelstan, king of the English. When news of Harald Fairhair's death in Norway reached England, Æthelstan gave Haakon ships and men for an expedition to claim his inheritance in Norway. Haakon gained popularity and support with the people and landowners of Norway by promising to give up the high taxes that his father Harald had put in place. As a result Erik lost all support and fled first to Orkney, and then to York (*Jórvík*).

Some accounts such as the sagas say that Erik was made a sub-king of Northumbria under Æthelstan's authority. However, English and Irish sources say that Erik became King of Northumbria after Æthelstan's death and in defiance of Æthelstan's brother Eadred, as part of what could be called a spirit of Northumbrian independence. For a long time Northumbria had been fought over between the Anglo-Saxons and the Norse-Gaels or 'sons of Ivar' (*Uí Ímair*) who ruled the Irish Sea, Dublin, the western coast of Scotland, the Hebrides, and some parts of Northern England.

The capital of Northumbria was York, founded by the Romans as *Eboracum*, called *Ebrauc* by the Britons, *Eoforwic* by the Anglo-Saxons, and when it was captured by the Great Heathen Army of Vikings under Ivar the Boneless in November 866 it was called *Jórvík* and became dominated by

---

[64] Snorri Sturluson, Heimskringla: The Saga of Harald Fairhair (Haralds Saga Hárfagra), c1220s, Iceland, Heimskringla.no, 2020,
<https://heimskringla.no/wiki/Haraldz_saga_ins_h%C3%A1rfagra_(FJ)> Accessed 17/02/2022

Norse warrior-kings. Version D of the *Anglo-Saxon Chronicle* tells us what happened when the Northumbrians selected Eric Bloodaxe as their king in 947:

"Her Eadred cyning oferhergode eall Norðhymbra land,
for þæm þe hi hæfdon genumen him Yryc to cyninge,
7 þa on þære hergunge wæs þæt mære mynster forbærnd æt Rypon þæt Sancte Wilferð getimbrede.
7 þa se cyning hamweard wæs, þa offerde se here innan Heoforwic,
wæs þæs cynges fyrde hindan æt Ceasterforda, 7 þær mycel wæl geslogon.
Ða wearð se cyning swa gram þæt he wolde eft in fyrdian 7 þone eard mid ealle fordon.
Þa Norðhymbra witan þæt ongeaton, þa forlæton hi Hyryc 7 wið Eadred cyning gebeton þa dæde". [65]

"This year Eadred the king ravaged all Northumberland,
because they had taken Erik to be their king,
and then, during the pillage, was the great minster burned at Ripon that St. Wilfrid built.
And as the king went homewards, then the army of York overtook him,
the rear of the king's forces was at Chesterford; and there they made great slaughter.
Then was the king so wroth that he would have marched his forces in again and wholly destroyed the land.
When the North-humbrian witan understood that, then forsook they Erik, and made compensation for".

Version E of the *Anglo-Saxon Chronicle* tells us that the Northumbrians once again took Erik as their king in 852, but this was short-lived and Erik was expelled again in 854. From then on York and Northumbria remained part of a united Anglo-Saxon kingdom.

852
"Her Norðhymbre fordrifan Anlaf Cyning 7 under fengon Yric Haroldes sunu".

"This year the Northumbrians expelled King Anlaf, and received Erik the son of Harold".

854
"Her Norðhymbre fordrifon Yric 7 Eadred feng to Norðhymbra rice". [66]

"This year the Northumbrians expelled Erik; and King Edred took to the government of the Northumbrians".

Erik was killed shortly afterwards in an ambush, along with his son Haeric and his brother Ragnald on the moors of Stainmore. Accounts mention his murder at the hands of Maccus, an agent acting on the orders of Oswulf Ealdulfing, the High Reeve of Bamburgh and a supporter of Eadred.

---

[65] Anglo-Saxon Chronicle (D, The Worcester Chronicle), 948: Cotton MS Tiberius B IV, ff. 3r- 86v 2021, 11th Century, London, British Library, 2012, f051r
<https://www.bl.uk/manuscripts/Viewer.aspx?ref=cotton_ms_tiberius_b_iv_f051r> Accessed 21/02/2022

[66] Anglo-Saxon Chronicle (E, The Peterborough Chronicle), 952 & 964: Laud misc. 636, 12th Century, Oxford, Bodleian Library, 2018, f036r <https://digital.bodleian.ox.ac.uk/objects/6272311c-058d-417a-8e21-05e463b4f1f9/surfaces/9dc138d3-ba0d-4bc8-a7ca-4af976487187/> Accessed 21/02/2022

18.   Harald Bluetooth: Uniting the Tribes

Harald 'Bluetooth' Gormsson (*Haraldr '*Blátǫnn' Gormsson*) was king of both Denmark from c958, and king of Norway from c970 until his death in c986. He was the son of Gorm the Old, and Thyra Dannebod (*Tanmarka But*). Harald introduced Christianity to Denmark and consolidated his rule over most of Jutland and Zealand. There are two theories as to the origin of the nickname 'Bluetooth', firstly that he had a noticeable bad tooth that was dark, the word 'blár' means 'blue', 'blue-black', or 'dark-coloured', alternatively he was called 'blue thane' or 'dark thane' in England, the Anglo-Saxon 'thegn' was then corrupted to 'tan' when it came back into Old Norse.

Harald also won power in Norway after the assassination of Harald II 'Greycloak' in c970. He had the help of an ally, the jarl Håkon Sigurdsson, whose father Sigurd Håkonsson had been killed by Harald Greycloak's men in c961. After a civil war between Håkon and Harald Greycloak's sons, in which Håkon was victorious, Håkon was then appointed by Harald Bluetooth to rule over Norway on his behalf as his vassal.

Harald Buetooth being baptized by Poppo (Poppa) the monk, c1200

Details of Harald's conversion to Christianity are conflicted. Widukind of Corvey (c973) claims that Harald was converted by a monk named Poppa, who demonstrated his faith by carrying a weight of iron heated by fire without being burned. Adam of Bremen (c1070) describes Harald being forcibly converted to Christianity by Holy Roman Emperor Otto I after being defeated in battle. Danish historian Saxo Grammaticus (c1208) states that Poppa's burning iron miracle was performed for Harald's son Sweyn Forkbeard who had doubts about his faith, while Harald converted to Christianity as part of a peace agreement with Otto I or Otto II. Snorri Sturluson (1179-1421) states that Harald was converted along with Jarl Håkon by Otto II (who ruled between 973 and 983).

After the death of Harald's mother Thyra, his father Gorm the Old had a Rune stone raised in the town of Jelling in Denmark in memory of his wife, describing her as the 'Pride of Denmark' or the 'Ornament of Denmark' (*tanmarka but*). When Gorm the Old died in around 958, Harald raised a stone in memory of both of his parents and in celebration his conquest of Denmark and Norway, and his conversion of the Danes to Christianity, thus securing his legacy. These two stones are referred to as the Jelling stones.

The larger Jelling stone inscription of Harald Bluetooth

ᚼᛅᚱᛅᛚᛏᚱ : ᚴᚢᛏᚢᚴᛦ : ᛒᛅᚦ : ᚴᛅᚢᚱᚢᛅ	haraltr : kunukʀ : baþ : kaurua
ᚴᚢᛒᛚ : ᚦᛅᚢᛋᛁ : ᛅᚠᛏ : ᚴᚢᚱᛘ ᚠᛅᚦᚢᚱ ᛋᛁᚾ	kubl : þausi : aft : kurm faþur sin
ᛅᚢᚴ ᛅᚠᛏ : ᚦᛅᚢᚱᚢᛁ : ᛘᚢᚦᚢᚱ : ᛋᛁᚾᛅ : ᛋᛅ	auk aft : þąurui : muþur : sina : sa
ᚼᛅᚱᛅᛚᛏᚱ (:) ᛁᛅᛋ : ᛋᛅᛦ • ᚢᛅᚾ • ᛏᛅᚾᛘᛅᚢᚱᚴ	haraltr (:) ias : sąʀ * uan * tanmaurk

ᛅᛚᛅ • ᛅᚢᚴ • ᚾᚢᚱᚢᛁᛅᚴ	ala * auk * nuruiak

• ᛅᚢᚴ • ᛏ(ᛅ)ᚾᛁ (• ᚴᛅᚱᚦᛁ •) ᚴᚱᛁᛋᛏᚾᛅ	* auk * t(a)ni (* karþi *) kristną

"Haraldr konungr bað gǫrva kumbl þausi	"King Haraldr ordered this monument made
aft Gorm faður sinn	after Gorm, his father,
auk aft Þórví móður sína.	and after Thyrvé, his mother;
Sá Haraldr es sér vann Danmǫrk alla	that Haraldr for himself won all of Denmark
auk Norveg auk dani gærði kristna".	and Norway and made the Danes Christian".

An aspect of Harald's legacy that he could not possibly have predicted is the wireless technology known as 'Bluetooth'. Originally developed by Swedish company Ericsson, it was given its name based on the idea that the technology would unite devices in the same way that Harald Bluetooth had united the tribes of Denmark. The Bluetooth symbol is a bindrune of his initials 'H' and 'B' in Younger Futhark runes:

   +   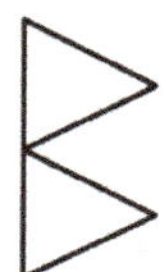   =   

19.   Egill Skallagrimsson: The Warrior Poet

Egill Skallagrimsson, 17th century manuscript

Egill Skallarimsson (*Egill Skallagrímsson*) was a 10th century warrior poet born in Iceland around 904. Much of what we know about him comes from the Sagas, particularly *Egill's Saga*, possibly written by Snorri Sturluson. He appears as something of an anti-hero who is full of contradictions, what some might describe as a 'complex character', or a 'product of his time'.

On one side of Egill's character is the poet, who composed his first poem at the age of three, going on to become celebrated and praised as the best poet of his time. Perhaps the most famous of Egil's poems is the *Lausavísur* (single verse) no.3 known as '*Þat mælti mín móðir*', which has been generally translated as 'My mother once told me':

<table>
<tr><td>

"Þat mælti mín móðir,
at mér skyldi kaupa
fley ok fagrar árar,
fara á brott með víkingum,
standa upp í stafni,
stýra dýrum knerri,
halda svá til hafnar
höggva mann ok annan".[67]

</td><td>

"It was told by my mother,
to me, I should buy
a ship and fair oars,
travel away with vikings,
stand up on the stern,
steer a dear ship,
hold so to the haven,
hew down a man or two".

</td></tr>
</table>

On the other side of Egill's character is the absolutely fearless beserker who had a capacity to kill, both with spontaneous and unpredictable outbursts of extreme violence, and with cold calculation.

Berserkers were a class of warriors who wore bear skins and worked themselves into a trance-like fury leading up to battle. The word 'berserk' or the phrase 'going berserk' in English comes from Old Norse, and is made up of '*serkr*' meaning 'shirt', and either '*bjǫrn*' meaning 'bear' or '*berr*' meaning

---

[67] Egill Skallagrimsson (poem), Snorri Sturluson (saga), Lausavísur (3) 'Þat mælti mín móðir': Chapter 40, Egill's Saga, 13th Century, Iceland, Netútgáfan (Online Version), 1998, <https://www.snerpa.is/net/isl/egils.htm> Accessed 22/02/2022

'bare' or 'naked'. The interpretation '*bare*-shirt' has been rejected in favour of '*bear*-shirt' or '*bear*-skin', especially since animal skins were also worn by wolf-warriors (*Úlfhéðnar*), and possibly wild-boar-warriors (*Jöfurr*).

At the age of seven, Egill was cheated during a game with some local boys, after which he went home, took an axe, returned to the group of boys, singled out the boy who had cheated him, and struck the axe into his head, splitting his skull to the teeth.

With such a temperament, Egill was involved in many a duel or '*holmgangr*', which at the time was a legally recognised way to settle a dispute. In Old Norse a '*holmr*' is a small island or islet on which such a duel would be fought, hence the term '*holmgangr*' meaning 'to go to an island' (to fight).

Egill became an enemy of Erik Bloodaxe after killing one of his men Bárðr of Atley in response to a grievous insult. Several orders to kill or capture Egill failed, resulting in those who were sent for him being killed.

When Erik took over the throne of Norway in around 933, he declared Egill an outlaw. Erik however was ousted from rule after one year by his brother Hákon the Good, fleeing first to Orkney and then ruling in *Jórvík* (York) in the Kingdom of Northumbria.

Egill later became shipwrecked on the coast of Northumbria and learned who ruled the land he had arrived on. He sought the help of his friend Arinbjörn and headed straight for Erik's court, where Arinbjörn argued Egill's case.

Egill, who faced execution, composed a special poem (*drápa*) in praise of Erik that was so astoundingly well composed, that Erik allowed him to live, even though Egill had killed his son.

Egill also fought in the service of King Æthelstan at the Battle of Brunanburh in 937 along with his brother Thorolf (*Þórólfr*) who died in the battle. Egill was awarded two chests of silver in compensation for the loss of his brother and for his service.

He then returned to his farm in Iceland and was well known as a force to be reckoned with in local matters. As he grew older he began to suffer increasing sight loss, but still kept his strength as an old man.

His last deed was to bury all of his treasure near Mosfellsbær, and when it was done, he killed the people who helped him bury his treasure, so that no one would ever know where it was buried. He died before Iceland adopted Christianity in around 995, aged approximately 90 or 91.

It could be argued that Egill's propensity towards extreme violence and murder was perhaps seen as necessary for survival in such wild and violent times, even something to be aspired to, in order to 'rise to the top' and navigate through the constant cycles of murder and revenge in early medieval history.

The Sagas were preserved in oral tradition for several centuries, passing through generations of storytellers before being written down, by which time some of the narratives had taken on differing degrees of Christian moral perspective, in contrast to the courtly romances of Western Europe at the same time in which stories had a clear moral.

The morality of Egil's Saga however is not so clear-cut. He appears to do bad things, perhaps for good reasons or old fashioned values, but going wildly over the top and out of control in the process, and he seems to get away with it.

20.   Erik the Red: Finding Greenland

Erik the Red from a woodcut in 1668

Erik Thorvaldsson (*Eiríkr Þórvaldsson*) was a Norse explorer, and the forst Norseman to permanently settle Greenland. He was known as 'Erik the Red' (*Eirirk Hinn Rauða*) either because of the colour of his hair and beard, or because of his fiery temper. He was born in Jæren, Norway in around 950, and when he was 10 years old, his father Thorvald Asvaldsson (*Þórvald Ásvaldsson*) was banished from Norway for manslaughter, and so the family left Norway and set sail west. They settled in *Hornstrandir* ('horn beaches') in northwestern Iceland.

Erik then moved to *Haukadalr* ('hawks dale') where he built a farm which was called *Eiríksstaðir* ('Erik's Place'). He married Thjodhild Jorunsdottir (*Þjódhild Jorundsdottir*) and they had a daughter named Freydis (*Freydís*), and three sons, Leif (*Leifr*), Thorvald (*Þórvaldr*), and Thorstein (*Þórsteinn*). Thjodhild and Leif had embraced Christianity, but Erik disliked it and remained a Norse Pagan. This was a source of disagreement between Erik and Thjodhild:

> *"Þjóðhildr vildi ekki samræði við Eirík, síðan hon tók trú, en honum var þat mjök móti skapi".*[68]

> "Thjodhild did not want to have intercourse with Erik since she had taken the faith, which went very much against his mood".

In 982 Erik was involved in a dispute with a farmer called Valthjof. Erik's thralls (slaves) accidentally started a landslide on Valthjof's farm, and in return Valthjof's friend Eyolf the Foul killed them. In retaliation, Erik killed Eyolf and Holmgang-Hrafn. The dispute was taken to a '*Þing*' ('assembly') and Erik was then banished from Haukadal.

Erik moved to the island of Oxney and asked a neighbour Thorgest to look after his *setstokkr*, special wooden beams or seat-posts usually decorated with carvings that his father had brought from Norway. When Erik had finished building his new house, he returned to Thorgest to retrieve the *setstokkr*, but

---

[68] Embleton, M. L. (Translator), Eiríks Saga Rauða (The Saga of Erik the Red):, Norse Text, Translation, and Word List, 2021, London, Independent, 2021, p.24, ISBN 979-8467805504

was unsuccessful in getting them back. It is not clear whether they simply could not be obtained because they had been misplaced or whether Thorgest had refused to give them back to him. Erik then found them at a place called Breidabolstad and took them, after which Thorgest chased him.

In the fight that followed Erik killed both Thorgest's sons and a few other men. The dispute was taken to another '*Þing*' ('assembly') and Erik was outlawed from Iceland for three years. Erik decided to set sail to find and explore new lands to settle

It was well known in Erik's time that a man named Gunnbjörn Ulfsson had discovered small islands west of Iceland after being blown off course by strong winds some time at the beginning of the 10th century. The islands he found had been named Gunnbjarnarsker ('Gunnbjorn's Skerries').

Snæbjörn Galti Hólmsteinsson was the first Norseman to intentionally navigate west to find these islands in 978. His attempts to settle on an inhospitable coast ended in disaster, brought about by bad weather, bad luck, and internal conflict. The Saga of this voyage has been lost over time.

Erik appears to have been better prepared for the journey and perhaps more lucky with the weather, successfully rounding the southern tip of the most southern of islands, now known as 'Cape Farewell' (*Nunap Isua*) on Egger Island (*Itilleq*).

He continued to explore the western coast of the land which seemed to have similar conditions to that of Iceland. When Erik returned to Iceland after his exile had ended, he spread the word about the new land that he called 'Greenland':

> *"Hann kallaði land þat, er hann hafði fundit, Grænland, því at hann kvað þat mundu fýsa menn þangat, ef landit héti vel".[69]*
>
> "He called the land which he had found Greenland, because as he said, it would attract people there if it was named well".

Erik's use of an attractive name worked, and people in Iceland living on poor land or those who had recently been hit by famine saw Greenland as an opportunity for a better life.

In 985 Erik led a group of settlers to Greenland, but the journey was treacherously difficult. 25 ships set off from Iceland, but only 14 arrived, the others being lost at sea or turning back.

Two colonies were established in Greenland, the Eastern Settlement (*Eystribyggð*, now Qaqortog), and the Western Settlement (*Vestribygð*, near modern day Nuuk). Erik settled in the Eastern Settlement and built the estate known as *Brattahlíð* ('steep slope' or 'broad slope' near Narsarsuaq) and was chieftain of all Greenland. He became wealthy and respected and the settlement flourished with up to 5,000 inhabitants.

Erik's son Leif had invited him to explore recently discovered lands to the west of Greenland that a man named Bjarni Herjólfson had seen but not explored. Erik was reluctant, but Leif had persuaded him to go along anyway. On their way to their ships, Erik was thrown from his horse, which he took as a sign that he was now too old to travel and that he would journey no further.

In 1002 a great sickness plagued Greenland, and Erik fell ill and died along with a large number of the population. Erik's settlement of Greenland paved the way for further explorations to the west and the Norse discovery of the American Continent.

---

[69] Embleton, M. L. (Translator), Grœnlendinga Saga (The Saga of the Greenlanders):, Norse Text, Translation, and Word List, 13th Century, London, Independent, 2021, p.7, ISBN 979-8464540590

The Norse settlement of Greenland survived until the arrival of what is now referred to as the Little Ice Age which began around 1420, after which many factors combined to bring about its decline and abandonment.

With the increase of ice and bad weather conditions, travel by sea became more dangerous and less frequent, which affected the the movement of people and the import and export of goods, which had also become increasingly taxed. Natural resources had become depleted and goods that Greenland had exported were now more easily obtainable elsewhere. Trade links collapsed and contact with Iceland and the other Scandinavian nations was lost.

In the 200 years since Christianity had been adopted, Christian attitudes to the indigenous peoples of Arctic and Subarctic Greenland, such as the Dorset and Thule people, viewed them as heathens or pagans and therefore culturally inferior. Conflicts between the two peoples arose, and the Norse population lost the opportunity to interact with them and learn how to survive and thrive in increasingly colder conditions, to which the indigenous peoples were very well adapted.

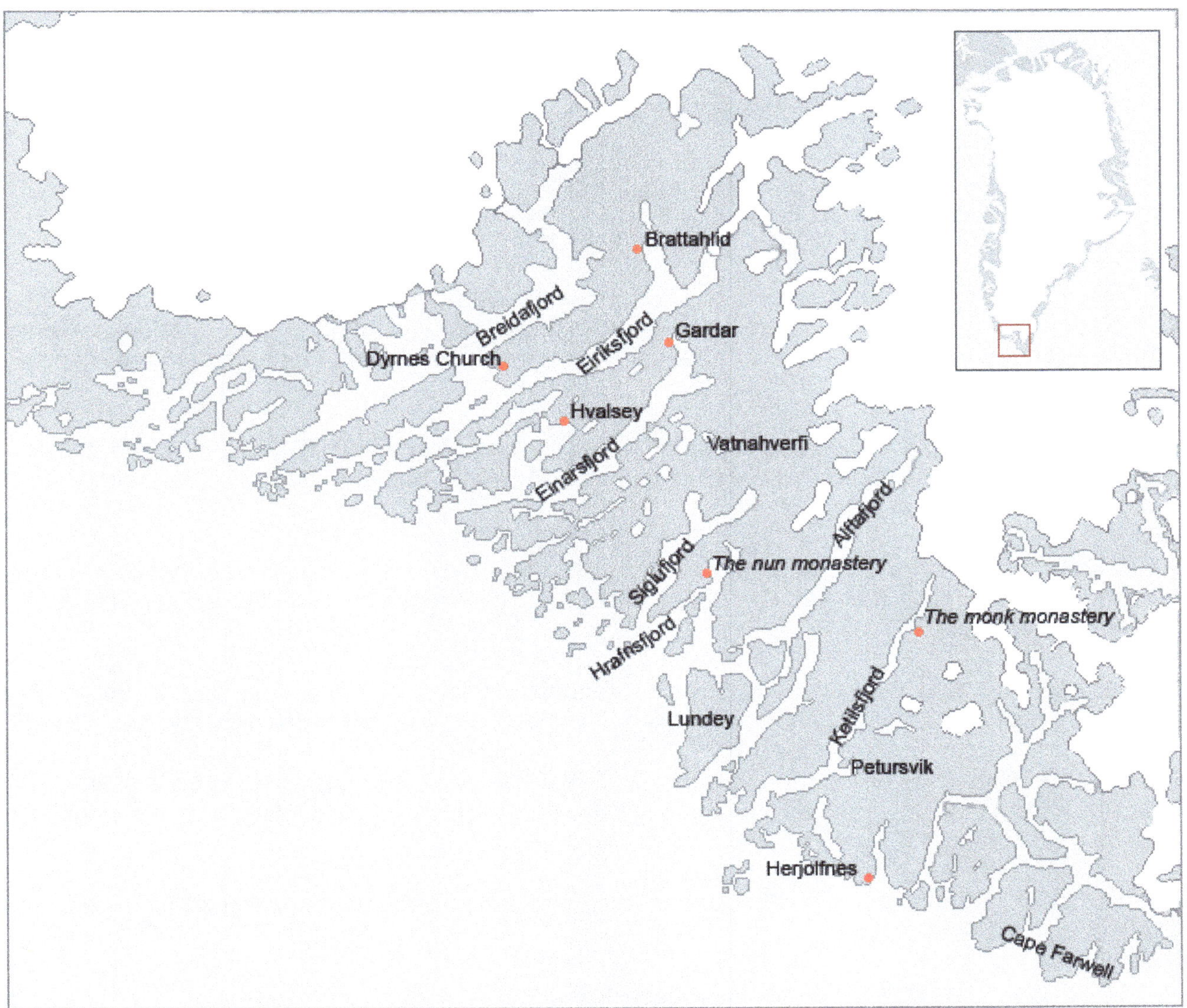

Eystribygð, the Eastern Settlement of Greenland

21.   Olaf Tryggvason: The Christian Conversion

The crowning of Olaf I of Norway by Peter Nicolai Arbo, 19th century

Olaf Tryggvason was born around 960 and later became King of Norway, ruling from 995 to 1000. He was the son of Tryggvi Olafsson, king of the Viken region of Norway, and the great-grandson of Harald Fairhair. His rule represents one of the significant periods during which the Norse people of Scandinavia were converted to Christianity.

Some sources say that Olaf was born in Orkney after his mother Astrid Eiriksdottir had fled there to escape his fathers' killers. Some sources however say that Olaf was already three years old when she fled to Orkney with him.

Olaf and his mother Astrid attempted to travel to Gardarike (Kyiv) where Astrid's brother Sigurd was in the service of Vladimir the Great. Olaf was three years old when they set sail on a merchant ship bound for Novgorod.

While in the Baltic Sea they were captured by Estonian Vikings and sold into slavery for six years before being rescued by Sigurd and finally taken to Novgorod to live under the protection of Vladimir.

Vladimir made Olaf chief of his men-at-arms, and Olaf became very popular with his soldiers, which Vladimir perceived as a threat to the safety of his reign, believing that Olaf could command their loyalty instead of his.

After this Vladimir's friendship with Olaf cooled, Olaf decided to seek his fortune elsewhere, and set off to go raiding in the Baltic Sea.

In 982 Olaf was caught in a particularly bad storm and forced to port in Wendland, the territory populated by the various Western Slavic tribes living near Germanic settlements.

Here he met Queen Geira, daughter of King Burislav, who ruled the part of Wendland where he had landed. She offered him and his men a place to stay for the winter. He began courting her and they soon married.

Olaf helped Geira to reclaim the baronies that had refused to submit to her rule and pay taxes, and he stayed in the country until her untimely death three years later.

A map showing West Slavic tribes making up the area known as 'Wendland'

Olaf was so distraught at Geira's death that he could no longer bear to be in Wendland and went raiding in Skåne and Gotland.

He became involved in an alliance with Otto II of the Holy Roman Emperor who had assembled an army of Saxons, Franks, Frisians, and Wends to fight the Norse Pagan Danes. Otto II and his armies, including Olaf, were successful in defeating the Danes under Harald Bluetooth and Jarl Håkon, and converted them to Christianity.

After a series of raids from Friesland to the Hebrides, Olaf landed on one of the Scilly Isles where he met a seer who told him that he would become a renowned king and accomplish celebrated deeds, bringing many men to faith and baptism. The seer told him that there would be a battle in which he would be almost mortally wounded, but would recover and become baptised. As the seer had prophesied, Olaf was attacked by a mutiny and was wounded but survived. He was baptised soon afterwards.

In 988 Olaf sailed to England where an assembly had been called by Queen Gyda, sister of Olaf Cuaran the King of Dublin. Gyda was the widow of an earl and was searching for a new husband. Of all the candidates that came, Gyda chose Olaf, even though he was wearing his bad weather clothes, and all the other men were dressed in their best finery. Gyda and Olaf married and spent half of their time in England, and the other half in Ireland.

In 995 there had been rumours of a king in Ireland with Norwegian blood, and so Jarl Håkon sent Thorer Klakka to Ireland posing as a merchant to find out what he could.

Thorer befriended Olaf, and rather than simply luring him to Norway so that Jarl Håkon could bring him under his power as Thorer had been instructed, Thorer told Olaf that Jarl Håkon was losing popularity in Norway and that he had been weakened by fighting with the Danish king because of his rejection of the Christian faith.

Olaf sailed to Norway and found that many men were already in revolt against Håkon who had hidden himself at a farm in a pigsty along with his slave Kark. Olaf and his men came to the farm where they were hiding and Olaf then made a speech offering a great reward for the mand who hilled Håkon.

Håkon became distrustful of his slave Kark who he feared would kill him for the reward. When Håkon fell asleep, Kark decapitated him. The next day Kark went to Olaf and presented Håkon's head to him, but instead of being rewarded, Kark was then decapitated himself.

Once Olaf had been confirmed as King of Norway, he began travelling to all the parts of Norway that had fallen under Danish rule, making them all swear allegiance to him and be baptised, which they did reluctantly.

Centuries earlier, when Emperor Charlemagne converted the Saxons to Christianity, his advisor Alcuin of York took issue with the conversions being 'on pain of death', arguing instead that they must be a matter of conscience. Charlemagne later abolished the death penalty for paganism in 797.

Olaf on the other hand had no such advice or counsel, and those who refused to be baptised were tortured with snakes, hot pokers, and hot coals, or executed.

He also baptised the explorer Leif Eriksson and sent a priest with him back to Greenland to convert the rest of the population there:

"Eitt sinn kom konungr at máli við Leif ok sagði: "Ætlar þú til Grænlands í sumar?"
"Þat ætla ek", sagði Leifr, "ef þat er yðvarr vili".
Konungr svarar: "Ek get, at þat muni vel vera, ok skaltu þangat fara með erendum mínum, at boða þar kristni".

"One time, the king spoke to Leif and said: "Do you intend to go to Greenland in summer?".
"That I do intend", said Leif, "If that is your will".
The king answered: "I do, for that will be well, and you shall travel there with my purpose, to preach there Christianity".

Leifr kvað hann ráða skyldu, en kveðst hyggja, at þat erendi myndi torflutt á Grænlandi.	Leif said that the king should decide that, but that he thought the errand would be difficult in Greenland.
Konungr kveðst eigi þann mann sjá, er betr væri til fallinn en hann, - "ok muntu giftu til bera".	The king said there was no one better for the task to fall to than him, "and luck shall carry you towards".
"Þat mun því at eins", segir Leifr, "ef ek nýt yðvar við".[70]	"That it should be", said Leif, "if I travel with your luck also".

Olaf's third wife was Tyra, the sister of Sweyn Forkbeard of Denmark, who had fled her heathen husband Burislav of Wendland.

In 1000, an expedition was undertaken to take back Tyra's lands from Burislav. However Olaf was met by the combined Swedish, Danish, and Wendish fleets, together with the fleet of Jarl Håkon's sons.

The Battle of Svolder, by Otto Sinding

In the battle that followed, known as the 'Battle of Svolder', Olaf fought to the last on his great ship known as *Ormrinn Langi* ('The Long Serpent') which was described as 'the mightiest ship in the North'. Finally he leapt overboard and was never seen again.

The folk ballad *Ormrinn Langi* ('The Long Serpent') tells the story of the Battle of Svolder. Written in Faroese, with several different versions, the most popular version was published in *Færøsk Anthologi* (Faroese Anthology) in 1846.

There were rumours that Olaf had survived his leap into the sea and had made his way to safety, with sightings in Rome and elsewhere in Europe, even as far away as Jerusalem, suggesting to some that Olaf had gone on a pilgrimage in his last days.

---

[70] Embleton, M. L. (Translator), Eiríks Saga Rauða (The Saga of Erik the Red):, Norse Text, Translation, and Word List, 2021, London, Independent, 2021, p.23, ISBN 979-8467805504

22.   Bjarni Herjolfsson: Finding Vinland

Bjarni Herjólfsson was a 10th century merchant who is believed to have been the first known European to discover the American continent, which he sighted some time between 986 and 999.

He was captain of a merchant ship based in Norway, and once a year he would sail to Iceland to visit his father Herjolf (*Herjólfr*).

One summer he sailed from Norway to Iceland, but on arrival discovered that his father had gone with Erik the Red to Greenland:

"Þat sama sumar kom Bjarni skipi sínu á Eyrar, er faðir hans hafði brot siglt um várit.

Þau tíðendi þóttu Bjarna mikil ok vildi eigi bera af skipi sínu.

Þá spurðu hásetar hans, hvat er hann bærist fyrir, en hann svarar, at hann ætlaði at halda siðvenju sinni ok þiggja at föður sínum vetrvist, "ok vil ek halda skipinu til Grænlands, ef þér vilið mér fylgð veita".

Allir kváðust hans ráðum fylgja vilja.

Þá mælti Bjarni: "Óvitrlig mun þykkja vár ferð, þar sem engi vár hefir komit í Grænlandshaf".[71]

"That same summer came Bjarni's ship to Eyrar, where his father had sailed from in the spring.

This news greatly affected Bjarni and he did not want to unload his ship.

His crew asked him what he wanted to do but he answered that he wanted to keep his custom of spending the winter with his father "and I want to sail to Greenland if you will follow me".

All of them said they would follow his counsel.

Then Bjarni said: "Our voyage will look unwise, since none of us have sailed the Greenland sea".

Bjarni and his crew set sail west from Iceland to go and find his father, but they were blown off course by a storm. As no one in Bjarni's crew had been to Greenland before, they had to search for it based on what they had heard described about the land.

Bjarni saw low lying hills covered with forests much further to the west. The land looked habitable, but Bjarni was focused on reaching Greenland to visit his father and was not as interested in exploring the land as his crew.

They eventually reached Greenland and Bjarni stayed with his father at a place that was since known as *Herjolfsnes* ('Herjolf's headland').

Bjarni visited Erik the Red and reported his findings, where he was criticised by some people for his lack of curiosity.

There was then much discussion throughout the Norse world about exploring this new land, and Erik's son Leif bought Bjarni's ship from him and set off to retrace Bjarni's journey.

Even though Bjarni himself may have lacked the curiosity of other Norse explorers, his discovery brought about a number of voyages to the American continent.

---

[71] Embleton, M. L. (Translator), Grœnlendinga Saga (The Saga of the Greenlanders):, Norse Text, Translation, and Word List, 13th Century, London, Independent, 2021, p.10, ISBN 979-8464540590

23.   Sweyn Forkbeard: The House of Denmark

Sweyn Forkbeard from a 13th century miniature

Sweyn 'Forkbead' Haraldson (*Sveinn Haraldsson Tjúguskegg*, *Swegen*) was a king of Denmark from 986 to 1014, king of Norway from 986 to 995, and then again from 1000 to 1014, and king of the English from 1013 to 1014. He was the son of Harald Bluetooth, and was baptised as 'Otto' in honour of the Holy Roman Emperor Otto I or Otto II. Some accounts say that his mother was called Gunnhild, whereas some say his mother was Tove from Western Wendland. Sweyn revolted against his father Harald and seized the throne from him in around 986. Harald was driven into exile and died that November.

Adam of Bremen depicted Sweyn as a pagan who rejected his baptism and his father's Christianity, persecuted Christians. Sweyn is also said to have built churches in Scania and Zealand, which does not seem to fit with the anti-Christian narrative that Adam of Bremen had attributed to him. Perhaps Adam of Bremen's view was partly formed by the fact that Sweyn had shunned the Archbishopric of Bremen in favour of English bishops instead who were less politically integrated into the state and therefore less of a threat to Sweyn's authority.

Perhaps in a time of religious change, like many others Sweyn struggled between Christianity and Paganism, which left room for Christian commentators to later narrate that he ultimately achieved his success only *after* had fully converted to and embraced Christianity. Sweyn was deposed in 995 or 996 by his father's allies and exiled to Scotland. Some saw this as his punishment from God for the uprising that had killed his father.

Olaf the Swede (*Olof Skötkonung*), Erik Håkonsson (*Eiríkr Hákonarson*), and the earls of Lade formed an alliance with Sweyn against Olaf Tryggvason culminating in the Battle of Svolder, and when Olaf Tryggvason's forces were defeated, Norway was divided up among the allies, with Sweyn regaining control of Viken in Norway.

In 1002, the English king Æthelred the Unready ordered a massacre of Danes who had settled in England. This could be said to be the motivation for Sweyn's involvement in frequent raids against England from 1002 to 1012.

Other historians argue that the motivation was purely the prospect of Danegeld, payments made to the Vikings to make them leave and to prevent them destroying the land. Such payments were only short term solutions, and only encouraged Vikings to return again and again for further payments, which for them became a tax or a form of tribute.

In 1013 Sweyn led an invasion of England, during which King Æthelred the Unready went into exile on the Isle of Wight and sent his sons Edward the Confessor (*Ēadpeard Andettere*) and Edward the Noble (*Ælfred Æþeling*) to Normandy. The *Anglo-Saxon Chronicle* describes Sweyn's invasion as follows:

"On þissum ilcan geare toforan þæm monðe Augustus com Swegen cyning mid his flotan to Sandwic,
7 wende swyðe hraðe abutan Eastenglum into Humbra muþan, 7 swa upweard andlang Trentan oð he com to Gæignesburh,
7 þa sona beah Uhtred eorl 7 ealle norðhymbre to him, 7 eall þæt folc on Lindesige, 7 siþþan þæt folc into Fifburgum,
7 raþe ðæs eall here benorðan Wætlingan stræte, 7 him man sealde gislas of ælcere scire.
Syþþan he undergeat þæt eall folc him to gebogen wæs, þa bed he þæt mon sceolde his here mettian 7 horsian,
7 he þa wende syþþan suðweard mid fulre fyrde, 7 betæhte þa scypu þa Cnute his suna,
7 syþþan he com ofer Wætlinga stræte worhton þæt mæste yfel þæt ænig here don mihte".[72]

"In this same year, before the month of August, came Sweyne the king with his fleet to Sandwich;
and went soon the road about East-Anglia into the Humber-mouth, and so upward along the Trent, until he came to Gainsborough.
and then soon submitted Utred the Earl, and all Northumbria to him, and all the folk in Lindsey, and afterwards the folk in the Five Boroughs,
and soon were all the army to the north of Watling-street; and him hostages were given him from each shire.
Since he understood that all folk to him subject were, then bid he that men should have provision and horses;
and he then went afterwards southward with his main army, the ships and the hostages to his son Knut.
And after he came over Watling-street, wrought they the most evil that any army might do".

On Christmas Day 1013, Sweyn was declared King of England, but lasted only five weeks before dying on the 3rd February 1014. His body was returned to Denmark and buried at either Roskilde or Lund. Sweyn's elder son Harald II became king of Denmark, while his younger son Canute (*Knútr*) was declared King of England by the Danelaw.

Sweyn's daughter Estrid Svendsdatter was the mother of King Sweyn II of Denmark, and her descendants continue to reign in Denmark to this day. In 1469, Margaret of Denmark married James III of Scotland, which reintroduced Sweyn's bloodline into the Scottish royal house. After James VI of Scotland inherited the throne of England in 1603, Sweyn's descendants were once again monarchs of England.

---

[72] Anglo-Saxon Chronicle (E, The Peterborough Chronicle), 952 & 964: Laud misc. 636, 12th Century, Oxford, Bodleian Library, 2018, f036r <https://digital.bodleian.ox.ac.uk/objects/6272311c-058d-417a-8e21-05e463b4f1f9/surfaces/4febf20b-483c-4222-be11-3ce439f72a99/> Accessed 24/02/2022

24.   Leif Eriksson: Finding Vinland

Leif Erikson by Hans Dahl (1849-1937)

Leif Eriksson (*Leifr Eiriksson*) was a Norse explorer who is believed to have been the first European to set foot on the American continent.

He was born between 970 and 980, the son of Erik the Red who founded the first Norse settlement of Greenland.

The two Sagas concerning Leif Erikson and the Norse discovery of the American Continent are *Grœnlendinga Saga* (The Saga of the Greenlanders), and *Eiríks Saga Rauða* (The Saga of Erik the Red), collectively known as *Vinlandssögur* (The Vinland Sagas) or *Vinlandingasögur* (The Sagas of the Vinlanders).

According to *Grœnlendinga Saga* it was Bjarni Herjolfsson who was blown off course on his way to Greenland where he saw new lands to the west but did not explore them. Afterwards Leif bought Bjarni's ship from him and retraced Bjarni's journey to explore the new lands.

According to *Eiríks Saga Rauða* it was Leif that was blown off course to explore new lands west of Greenland on his way back from Norway, where King Olaf Tryggvason had baptised him and instructed him to convert Greenland to Christianity.

Leif then named three lands, the first being characterised by large stone slabs which he called *Helluland* ('slab land'), the second land was flat with thick forests which he called *Markland* ('forest land'), and they went to shore on the third land:

"Ok gengu þar upp ok sást um í góðu veðri ok fundu þat, at dögg var á grasinu, ok varð þeim þat fyrir, at þeir tóku höndum sínum í döggina ok brugðu í munn sér ok þóttust ekki jafnsætt kennt hafa sem þat var".[73]	"And went they up to the shore and looked about, in fine weather they found dew on the grass, that they took in their hands, and brought to their mouths, and they thought nothing was as sweet as that was".

When they discovered vines of wild grapes on the third land, he called it *Vínland*, which has been translated as 'vine' or 'wine' land, but some scholars have suggested that there is in fact a short vowel 'i' in *Vinland* which suggests the name 'pasture' or 'meadow' land.

Leif and his crew set up a camp called *Leifsbúða* ('Leif's Booths' or 'Leif's Camp') which is believed to be the site discovered at L'Anse aux Meadows, the northernmost tip of Newfoundland and Labrador. They gathered grapes, vines, and timber for their return cargo:

Svá er sagt, at eftirbátr þeira var fylldr af vínberjum.	So it was said that their boat was filled with grapes.
Nú var höggvinn farmr á skipit.	Now they cut down wood as cargo for the ship.
Ok er várar, þá bjuggust þeir ok sigldu burt, ok gaf Leifr nafn landinu eftir landkostum ok kallaði Vínland, sigla nú síðan í haf, ok gaf þeim vel byri, þar til er þeir sá Grænland ok fjöll undir jöklum".[74]	And when spring came, they made ready and sailed away, and Leif named the land after its features and called it *Vínland*, they now sailed to sea, and they were given fair wind until they saw Greenland and the mountains under glaciers".

On Leif's return journey he spotted Thorir and his crew who had been shipwrecked on a rock. After rescuing them he was then given the nickname Leif 'the Lucky' (*Leifr hinn Heppni*). The Germanic concept of luck or *hamingja* was different from that of modern times. Everyone was believed to possess an indeterminable amount of luck as an intangible quality. Leif's younger brothers attempted to emulate his success, but sadly they were not as lucky.

Leif's brother Thorvald explored west and east from Leif's camp, but broke his ship's keel on a peninsula which was then named *Kjalarnes* ('Keel Point'). There followed a conflict with natives, who the Norsemen called *Skrælingr* ('skin wearers' or 'barbarians'), and after a battle in which the Norsemen were outnumbered but fought them off, Thorvald was fatally wounded by a stray arrow and died shortly afterwards. He requested that he be buried on the headland with a cross above him. The headland was then called *Krossanes ('Cross Point')*. Thorvald's crew then returned to Greenland.

Leif's brother Thorstein attempted to sail to Vinland so that he could find and retrieve Thorvald's body at Krossanes. He travelled with his wife Gudrid and a crew of 25 men. They were driven about by bad weather, eventually arriving at Lysufjord in the Western Settlement of Greenland where they sought shelter with families living there. A sickness then struck the settlement and Thorstein and many others died.

---

[73] Embleton, M. L. (Translator), Grœnlendinga Saga (The Saga of the Greenlanders):, Norse Text, Translation, and Word List, 13th Century, London, Independent, 2021, p.15, ISBN 979-8464540590
[74] Embleton, M. L., 2021, p.17

25.   Freydis Eriksdottir: The Vinland Villainess

Freydís Eiríksdóttir is described in *Eiríks Saga Rauða* as the illegitimate daughter of Erik the Red and half-sister of Leif, Thorvald, and Thorstein Eriksson. She is portrayed as a brave and protective Viking warrior who joined Thorfinn Karlsefni's expedition to *Vínland.* She demonstrated her bravery during an attack by the native *Skrælingjar* with war-slings and catapults. The Norsemen had never seen such weapons before, and this caused panic and confusion, which Freydis criticised:

"Hví rennið þér undan þessum auvirðismönnum, svá gildir menn sem þér eruð, er mér þætti sem þér mættið drepa niðr svá sem búfé? Ok ef ek hefða vápn, þætti mér sem ek skylda betr berjast en einnhverr yðvar".[75]

"Why are you running away from such unworthy opponents? such men that you are, who look to me like you could kill them as easily as livestock, and if I had a weapon I would fight them better than any of you".

Freydis, who was 8 months pregnant, picked up the sword of Thorbrand Snorrisson who had been killed, and then screamed at the natives while slapping the sword against one of her breasts. This frightened them and they retreated to their boats and fled. Karlsefni and the others praised her zeal.

Grœnlendinga Saga paints a very different picture. She made a joint-venture deal with brothers Helgi and Finnbogi to go to Vinland and share half of all the profit that they made from their cargo. Freydis immediately broke the agreement by smuggling extra men into her ship. The brothers arrived in *Vínland* first and set up at Leif's Camp. When Freydis arrived she ordered the brothers to move their supplies out of Leif's booths, because they were intended for her, not them. This would be the first of many disagreements between Freydis and the brothers who set up a separate camp.

Freydis eventually went to their hut and so began a conversation that was intended to look like an attempt to make peace between them, but when Freydis returned to her husband, she claimed that Helgi and Finnbogi had beaten her, and that unless he would exact revenge upon them she would divorce him. He immediately gathered his men and did as she told him:

"Nú váru þar allir karlar drepnir, en konur váru eftir, ok vildi engi þær drepa.
Þá mælti Freydís: "Fái mér öxi í hönd".

Svá var gert.
Síðan vegr hon at konum þeim fimm, er þar váru, ok gekk af þeim dauðum".[76]

"Now all the men were killed, there remained the women, but no one wanted to kill them.
Then Freydis said: "Give me the axe in my hand".
So was it done.
Then she slayed the five women who were there, and all of them were dead".

Freydis threatened to kill anyone who spoke of these events, insisting instead that they should all agree on the story that Helgi and Finnbogi had decided to stay in Vinland. Word eventually reached her brother Leif who had three of Freydis's crew tortured until they told him everything. Leif disapproved of what his Freydis had done, but could not bring himself to punish her. He said instead that Freydis and her descendants would not thrive or do well, and she was shunned by everyone.

---

[75] Embleton, M. L. (Translator), Eiríks Saga Rauða (The Saga of Erik the Red):, Norse Text, Translation, and Word List, 2021, London, Independent, 2021, p.43, ISBN 979-8467805504
[76] Embleton, M. L. (Translator), Grœnlendinga Saga (The Saga of the Greenlanders):, Norse Text, Translation, and Word List, 13th Century, London, Independent, 2021, p.37, ISBN 979-8464540590

26. Canute the Great: The North Sea Emperor

Canute the Great, from a manuscript, c1031

Canute the Great, from a manuscript c1320

Canute (*Cnut*, *Knútr*) also known as Canute the Great (*Knútr inn Ríki*) was the son of Sweyn Forkbeard who became King of England from 1016 to 1035, King of Denmark from 1018 to 1035, and King of Norway from 1028 to 1035. These three kingdoms under Canute's rule are collectively referred to as the 'North Sea Empire', or the 'Anglo-Scandinavian Empire'.

Knýtlinga Saga (The Saga of Cnut's Descendants) written by Snorri Sturluson's nephew Olaf Thordarson (*Óláfr Þórðarson*) in the model of *Heimskringla* described him as follows:

"Knútr var manna mestr vexti ok sterkr at afli, manna fríðastr, nema nef hans var þunt ok eigi lágt ok nökkut bjúgt; hann var ljóslitaðr, fagrhárr ok mjök hærðr; hverjum manni var hann betr eygðr, bæði fagreygðr ok snareygðr".[77]

"Knut was of men the most grown and strong of means, the fairest of men, except that his nose was thin and not low and somewhat curved; he was light-coloured, fair-haired, and much hairy; to each man he was better eyed, both fair eyed and quick-eyed".

Canute's Danish conquest of England was concluded in the Battle of Assandun on the 18th October 1016. Canute and the Danish forces defeated the English king Edmund Ironside and his forces, and in the resulting peace negotiations, all of England north of the Thames belonged to Canute, and all of England to the south of the Thames belonged to Edmund until his death, after which it passed to Canute.

Edmund died shortly afterwards on the 30th of November, leading some people to suspect that he had been murdered, but the true circumstances of his death would never be known. The West Saxons accepted Canute as their king and he was crowned in London in 1017.

---

[77] Óláfr Þórðarson, Knýtlinga Saga (The Saga of Cnut's Descendants):, c1250s, Iceland, Heimskringla.no, 2020, <http://www.heimskringla.no/wiki/Knytlinga_saga> Accessed 26/02/2022

Edmund Ironside (left) and Canute the Great (right) at the battle of Assandun,
from the *Chronica Majora* ('Major Chronicle') by Matthew Paris
Corpus Christi College Cambridge MS. 26, fol. 80v, 14th century

When Canute became king of Denmark in 1018, he sought to unite the Danes and the English under a shared wealth and prosperity, enforced by the brutal punishment of anyone who sought to undermine him. After a decade of conflict with opponents in Scandinavia, Canute claimed the throne of Norway in Trondheim in 1028.

Canute's influence over the English and Danish churches and bishoprics rivalled that of the Archdiocese of Hamburg and Bremen, which gave Canute a degree of prestige and leverage within the Catholic Church. In 1027 Canute was invited to attend the coronation of the Holy Roman Emperor Conrad II in Rome by Pope John XIX. It was an incredibly prestigious event to be invited to, and it signalled that Canute the Great had 'arrived'.

Canute was generally thought of as a wise and successful king of England, which is possibly in part due to his treatment of the church. It was the people of the church wrote historic records which became the sources of later writings about him. In Henry of Huntingdon's *Historia Anglorum* ('History of the English') written a century later, there is the now famous story of Canute and the tide:

"Cum maximo vigore imperii, sedile suum in littore maris, cum ascenderet, statui jussit.

"With the greatest vigor of his empire, he ordered his seat to be placed on the shore of the sea when he was ascending.

Dixit autem mari ascendenti "Tu meæ ditionis est; et terra in qua sedeo mea est: nec fuit qui impune meo resisteret imperio. Imperio igitur tibi ne in terram mean ascendas, nec vestes nec membra dominatoris tui madefacere præsumas".

And he said to the rising sea, "You are under my jurisdiction; and the land in which I sit is mine; there is no one who could with impunity resist my rule. Therefore, do not mean to command yourself to ascend to the earth, and do not presume to dampen the clothes or limbs of your ruler".

Mare vero de more conscendens pedes regis et crura sine reverentia madefecit.

The sea habitually ascended, and the feet of the king and his legs without reverence drenched.

Rex igitur resiliens ait: "Sciant omnes habitantes orbem, vanam et frivolam regnum esse potentiam, nec regis quempiam nomine dignum præter Eum, cujus nutui coelum, terra, mare, legibus obeduint æternis".
Rex igitur Cnut nunquam postea coronam auream cervici suæ imposuit, sed super imaginem Domini, quæ cruci affixa erat, posuit eam in æternem, in laudem Dei Regis magni ; cujus misericordia Cnut regis anima quiete fruatur".[78]

The king then echoed saying: "Know all the inhabitants of the world, vain and frivolous is the power of kings, nor is anyone else the name worth besides him, by whose nods, heaven, land, and sea, his laws obeys in eternity.
The king therefore Canute never afterwards the crown of gold on his neck imposed, but on the image of the lord, which a cross affixed was forever, in praise of God the king, whose mercy Canute the king enjoyed his soul peace".

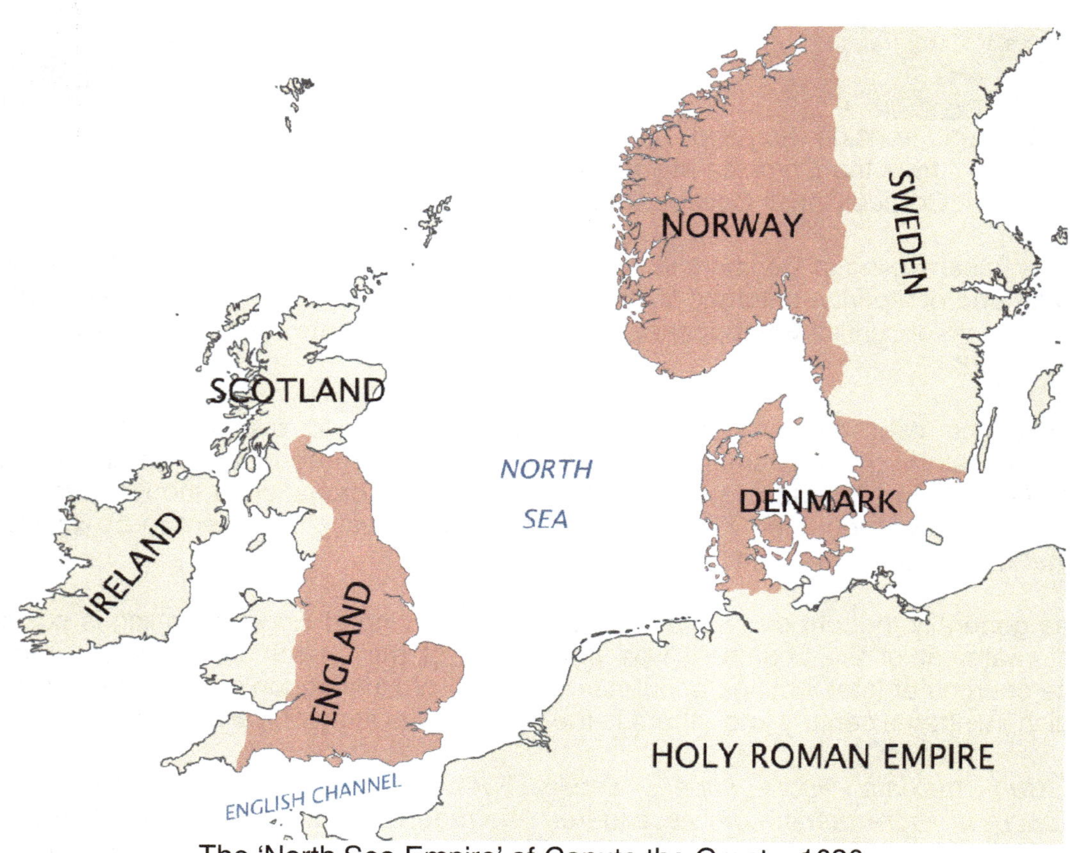

The 'North Sea Empire' of Canute the Great, c1030

Canute died on the 12th of November 1035 at Shaftesbury in Dorset and was buried in the Old Minster Cathedral in Winchester. After the Norman conquest of England in 1066 Old Minster was replaced by the present Winchester Cathedral, and Canute's remains were moved to a special mortuary chest there.

---

[78] Henry of Huntingdon, Thomas Arnold M.A. (Editor), Historia Anglorum (The History of the English):, 1154, London, Longman & Co., 1879, 2009, p.189
<https://archive.org/details/henriciarchidia00unkngoog/page/n265/mode/2up> Accessed 26/02/2022

27.   Thorfinn Karlsefni: Finding Vinland

A statue of Thorfinn Karlsefni by Einar Jonsson, 1918

Thorfinn 'Karlsefni' Thórdarson (*Þorfinn 'Karlsefni' Þórdarson*) was an Icelandic explorer who followed Leif Eriksson's route to *Vínland* with the hope of establishing a permanent Norse settlement there in around 1010. The nickname 'Karlsefni' has been variously translated as 'the makings of a man', 'a promising man' or 'a thorough man'. He was a successful merchant from Reynines, Skagafjord, in the north of Iceland. He married Gudrid Thorbjornadottir (*Guðríðr Þorbjarnardóttir*), and their son Snorri was the first European to have been born on the American Continent.

On arrival in *Vínland* they did a great deal of exploring the land, cutting timber, harvesting grapes, catching fish, hunting for game, and trading with the natives (*Skraelings*). Among the livestock they had brought with them was a bull, which frightened the natives and caused them to flee.

"Graðungr tók at belja ok gjalla ákafliga hátt.
En þat hræddust Skrælingar ok lögðu undan með byrðar sínar, en þat var grávara ok safali ok alls konar skinnavara, ok snúa til bæjar Karlsefnis ok vildu þar inn í húsin, en Karlsefni lét verja dyrrnar.

Hvárigir skilðu annars mál.
Þá tóku Skrælingar ofan bagga sína ok leystu ok buðu þeim ok vildu vápn helzt fyrir, en Karlsefni bannaði þeim at selja vápnin".[79]

"The bull took to bellowing and snorting very loudly.
Then this frightened the Skraelings and they ran away with their burdens, which included grey skins, sables, and all kinds of fur, they turned towards Karlsefni's farm and wanted to get into the house, but Karlsefni had protected the door.
Neither knew the others' language.
Then the Skraelings took off their bags and opened them, offering their goods, preferably in exchange for weapons, but Karlsefni forbade them to trade weapons".

---

[79] Embleton, M. L. (Translator), Grœnlendinga Saga (The Saga of the Greenlanders):, Norse Text, Translation, and Word List, 13th Century, London, Independent, 2021, p.30, ISBN 979-8464540590

The natives had also been offered milk based products which made them ill because they were lactose intolerant, and believing that they had been poisoned conflict arose between them. Conflict also occurred as a result of one of the natives attempting to take weapons in return for their goods, for which he was killed by one of Karlsefni's men. A large battle followed in which they were attacked on all sides by the natives, and according to *Eiríks Saga Rauða*, Freydis Eriksdottir scared them away by screaming at them and slapping a sword against her breast. After the battle, and realising that they were outnumbered by the natives, Karlsefni decided that they should leave the settlement in the spring and return to Greenland.

"At vári þá lýsir Karlsefni, at hann vill eigi þar vera lengr ok vill fara til Grænlands.
Nú búa þeir ferð sína ok höfðu þaðan mörg gæði í vínviði ok berjum ok skinnvöru.
Nú sigla þeir í haf ok kómu til Eiríksfjarðar skipi sínu heilu ok váru þar um vetrinn".[80]

"In the spring, Karlsefni declared that he did not wish to be there any longer and wished to travel to Greenland.
Now they prepared for their journey and they had much good quality vines, berries, and skins.
Now they sailed to sea and their ship came safely to Eriksfjord and they stayed there over the winter".

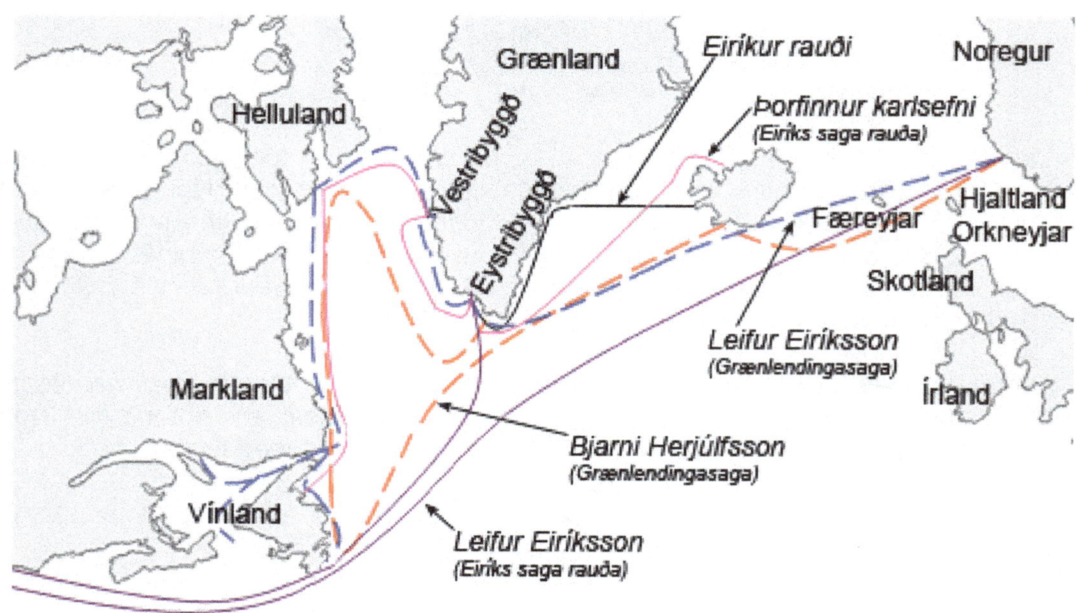

A map of the voyages to *Vínland*

After spending the winter in Greenland, Karlsefni returned with his wife Gudrid to his farm at Reynines, Skagafjord, Iceland.

There are many differences in the accounts given in *Grœnlendinga Saga* and *Eiríks Saga Rauða*, with the latter of the two seemingly conflating events in order to increase Thorfinn's role in the saga. This is perhaps because Haukr Erlendsson who compiled the *Hauksbók* in which *Eiríks Saga Rauða* is found, was a descendent of Thorfinn and wished to add to his ancestor's fame.

---

[80] Embleton, M. L. (Translator), Grœnlendinga Saga (The Saga of the Greenlanders):, Norse Text, Translation, and Word List, 13th Century, London, Independent, 2021, p.33, ISBN 979-8464540590

28.   Olaf II of Norway: Saint of the North

A statue of Olaf at Austevoll Church, Norway

Olaf II Haraldsson (*Ólafr Haraldsson*) was King of Norway between 1015 and 1028. During his lifetime he was known as *Ólafr Digri* (Olaf 'the Stout' or Olaf 'the Big'). His determination to convert the people of Norway to Christianity by any means necessary also earned him the nickname Olaf 'the Lawbreaker'. Like other Christianising kings of the medieval period, including his namesake Olaf Tryggvason, the techniques used to convert subjects were in some cases less about persuasion and conscience than brute force.

Olaf was born in around 995 and at the age of 16 was believed to have taken part in the Siege of Canterbury in 1011 alongside Thorkell the Tall. In 1008 he sailed to the southern coast of Finland to go raiding but was ambushed and almost killed by the Finns at what would be known as the Battle at Heralder (possibly modern day Uusimaa).

Skaldic poetry suggests that Olaf assisted Æthelred the Unready in repelling the Danes after the Viking attack on London Bridge. After the death of Sweyn Forkbeard in 1014, Harald II of Denmark took the throne of England. The Vikings and the people of the Danelaw elected Canute the Great as their king instead, while the English nobility recalled Æthelred from exile in Normandy to take the throne. Æthelred raised an army against Canute, which included Olaf, and drove the Danes out of England. Canute returned some months later, eventually becoming King of England in 1016. By this time Olaf had been baptised in Rouen while visiting Richard II of Normandy and had set his sights on Norway.

Arriving in Norway in 1015 Olaf declared himself king. His ambition was to unite Norway into one kingdom as Harald Fairhair had previously done. He won the support of the petty kings of the Uplands, and defeated Earl Sweyn, becoming the *de facto* ruler of Norway. Olaf's subjugation of the aristocracy caused them to support the invasion of Canute, and Olaf was driven into exile in the Kyivan Rus'. He spent his time there baptising many locals before being killed in the Battle of Stiklestad by forces loyal to Canute. In 1164 Pope Alexander III confirmed Olaf as a universally recognised saint of the Roman Catholic Church with the title *Rex Perpetuus Norvegiae* ('perpetual' or 'eternal king of Norway'). Olaf's canonisation as a saint encouraged the widespread adoption of Christianity by Scandinavians, and to this day he is a symbol of Norwegian independence.

29.   Harthacnut: The Last Danish King of England

Harthacnut, from a 14th century miniature

Harthacnut was born around 1017 and was the son of Canute the Great and his second wife Emma of Normandy. At the age of around 6, Harthacnut and his mother Emma were involved in the ceremonial movement of the body of Saint Ælfheah from London to Canterbury. Such a ceremony was seen by many as formal recognition of Harthacnut's place in the line of succession to the English throne.

In 1028 at the age of around 11, Harthacnut was placed on the throne of Denmark to rule on Canute's behalf, and his half-brother Svein was placed on the throne of Norway. Svein's heavy taxation and shunning of the Norwegian nobility in favour of Danish advisers made him unpopular, and when Magnus the Good invaded Norway in 1035, Svein fled to Harthacnut's court. Harthacnut did not believe he had the resources to invade and reclaim Norway, and soon afterwards they learned of the death of their father Canute.

Magnus the Good took full control of Norway, Harthacnut became king of Denmark, and Harthacnut's half-brother Harold Harefoot became King of England until his death in 1040, after which Harthacnut became King of England. The English had become accustomed to the king ruling in council, whereas Harthacnut was used to a much more autocratic style of ruling, which he would not change, particularly as he did not trust the ruling earls. His reign brought high taxes which coincided with poor harvest creating poverty and hardship followed by riots.

On the 8th June 1042, Harthacnut attended the wedding of the Danish thegn Tovi the Proud and his bride Gytha of Anglo-Saxon nobility. After consuming large quantities of alcohol drinking to the health of the bride, he collapsed, convulsed, and died. It was believed to have been a stroke brought about by an excessive intake of alcohol, but some believe that he was poisoned in a plot possibly organised by Edward the Confessor.

After his death Magnus the Good took the throne of Denmark, and Harthacnut's step-brother Edward the Confessor became King of England. Harthacnut was the last Danish king to rule in England.

30.   Harald Hardrada: The Last Invader

Harald (left) arriving near York, 13th century manuscript

Harald Hardrada Sigurdsson (*Haraldr Harðráði Sigurðarson*) was king of Norway from 1047 until his death in 1066. The nickname 'Hardrada' means literally 'hard ruler'. At the age of 15 Harald fought alongside his half-brother Olaf Haraldsson (later Saint Olaf) to reclaim the throne of Norway from Canute the Great. They were defeated by forces loyal to Canute, Olaf was killed, and Harald was exiled to the Kyivan Rus' (*Garðaríki*). He spent some time there as a mercenary in the army of Grand Prince Yaroslav the Wise, reaching the rank of Captain.

In 1034 he joined the Varangian Guard of the Byzantine Empire where he rose to the rank of commander and fought in Asia Minor, Bulgaria, Constantinople, Sicily, the Holy Land, and the Mediterranean. He earned a great deal of wealth during this time which he transported to Yaroslav in the Kyivan Rus' for safekeeping. In 1042 Harald left the Byzantine Empire to collect his wealth and begin his campaign to reclaim the Norwegian throne.

The Norwegian throne had passed from the Danes to Olaf his brother's illegitimate son Magnus the Good. Harald joined forces with Sweyn II of Denmark who intended to claim the Danish throne from Magnus. Magnus refused to fight his uncle and agreed to share the kingship with Harald, and in return Harald would share his wealth with him. The co-rule ended after a year when Magnus died, and Harald became the sole ruler of Norway, crushing all opposition. He then turned on his former ally Sweyn and claimed the Danish throne. His raids and campaigns were successful, but he never managed to conquer Denmark and renounced his claim.

In early 1066 Tostig Godwinson the former Earl of Northumbria and brother of the new English King Harold Godwinson pledged his allegiance to Harald and invited him to claim the English throne. Harald invaded with 10,000 troops and 300 longships, raiding the coast and defeating the forces of Northumbria and Mercia in the Battle of Fulford. Harold Godwinson led a surprise attack at Stamford Bridge on the 25th September, killing Harald and wiping out almost his entire army.

The death of King Harald Hardrada of Norway ended any hope of reviving the North Sea Empire of Canute the Great, and is seen by many historians as either the end of the Viking Age, or the beginning of the end.

31.   William the Conqueror: The Rise of the Normans

William the Conqueror, 13th century manuscript

William the Conqueror (William of Normandy) was the great-great-great-grandson of Rollo of Normandy. He was the son of Robert I and his mistress Herleva, and his illegitimate status resulted in the nickname 'William the Bastard'. After the death of Robert I in 1035 William was proclaimed Duke of Normandy at the age of 7 or 8. Norman noblemen began fighting among themselves, some seeking to influence and control William, some trying to kill him.

Before Robert I died he had placed William under the protection of Robert II Archbishop of Rouen which lasted until the Archbishop's death in 1037. Several attempts on William's life ultimately failed, and his rise to power began. In 1051 William travelled from Normandy to visit his cousin Edward the Confessor, King of England, and William claimed that Edward had promised that he should succeed him on the English throne. In 1064 Harold Godwinson the Earl of Wessex had made a trip to Normandy, and William claimed that Harold had also promised to support his claim to the English throne. In January 1066 Edward the Confesor died and Harold Godwinson was crowned shortly afterwards.

William assembled an invading force and successfully crossed the English Channel on the 28th September. Harold Godwinson, who had recently defeated Harald Hardrada at the Battle of Stamford Bridge in York, marched south to East Sussex, and on the 14th October the Battle of Hastings resulted in Norman victory. William was crowned King of England on Christmas day 1066. After putting down numerous rebellions, and having to pay and feed many soldiers at great cost, Willam needed records of what he was owed as king. He ordered a great survey of all England including population, land ownership, value, etc. The result was the Domesday Book which was finished in 1086.

The Normans replaced the Anglo-Saxons as the ruling class of England, and lands were passed from Anglo-Saxon to Norman ownership. The Nobility of England became part of a Norman culture and many of them owned lands on both sides of the channel. The Anglo-Norman language became distinct from the French that was being spoken in Paris, and some of it influenced the Old English language bringing about the shift to Middle English.

32.   Snorri Sturluson: Icelandic Historian

Snorri Sturluson by Christian Krohg, c1890s

Snorri Sturluson was an Icelandic historian, poet, lawyer, and politician. He was elected as lawspeaker of the Icelandic parlament in 1215 and served for three years before leaving Iceland for a royal invitation to Norway at the court of Hákon IV. He was interested in history and culture, and it was here that he gained an insight into the history of the Swedish and Norwegian kings.

His works are among the most important in Scandinavian history and saga tradition. He is believed to have authored or compiled much of the *Edda* (today known as the Prose Edda), which based on the original collection of poems known as the Poetic Edda, is the fullest and most detailed source of knowledge about Norse mythology.

Snorri also wrote *Heimskringla*, a collection of sagas outlining the history of the Swedish and Norwegian kings, beginning with the legendary dynasty of the Ynglings and continuing until the 12th century. He used a wide range of sources to write the sagas, including the materials he had collected during his trips to Norway and Sweden. Because of his distinctive style, Snorri is also thought to have been the author of Egil's Saga.

In 1220 Snorri returned to Iceland and was elected lawspeaker in 1222 on account of his fame as a poet. He remained in the position until 1232. He was a strong supporter of union with Norway which earned him enemies with the chieftains of Iceland. Snorri became the most powerful of the Icelandic chieftains and seemed to be consolidating power over all of the others in order to be able to offer Iceland to King Hákon.

A period of clan fighting in Iceland followed. Hákon intervened by inviting all of the chieftains to a peace conference in Norway, which some saw as a transparent attempt to lure them into a trap. Snorri returned to Norway to find that Hákon had lost faith in his reliability. He was ordered to stay in Norway, which he disobeyed returning to Iceland in 1239. He was assassinated by the chieftain Gissur Thorvaldsson (*Gissur Þorvaldsson*) and his men on the orders of King Hákon. It was stated by Hákon that if he had surrendered he would have been spared. With Hákon's influence over the chieftains, the Althing ratified a union with Norway and royal authority was instituted in Iceland by sworn oath. Absolute and hereditary monarchy was formally accepted in Iceland in 1662.

33.   The End

There are several events and factors that historians have used to mark the end of the Viking Age, political, military, economic, and cultural.

Some argue that it was the Christianisation of Scandinavia that brought an end to the Viking raids, but this was a long and gradual process. Vikings had been converted to Christianity during their travels as early as the 9th century, and brought their new religion home with them.

Kings were instrumental in Christianising the nations of Scandinavia, partly motivated by their personal beliefs, and partly because it offered the opportunity to do business with the increasingly wealthy Christian nations of Europe, something they had previously been barred from.

Harald Bluetooth declared Denmark a Christian nation in 975, and Iceland declared Christianity as the new religion by law in the year 1000. St Olaf's canonisation as a saint by local clergy in 1031 encouraged the widespread adoption of Christianity by Scandinavians. Denmark, Norway, and Sweden also established their own Archdioceses reporting directly to the Pope in 1104, 1154, and 1164 respectively.

The death of the last Scandinavian kings who ruled lands outside their native origin by conquest were also seen as the conclusion of a powerful struggle of rival dynasties. Harthacnut, the last king of the Danish House of Knýtlinga died in 1042, and was the last Danish king to rule in England.

The return of lands that had previously been occupied by Norse earls and kings concluded many territorial interests originally gained from Viking expansion. Scotland regained the Western Isles and the Isle of Man in 1266, and Orkney and Shetland from the King of Norway in 1469.

The rapid hit-and-run tactics that had initially made the Vikings so unpredictable and fearsome had given way to larger and larger armies met face to face on the battlefield. Their opponents increased their defences based on knowledge of the Vikings attacking strategies, and battlefield technology continually evolved.

In 1066 the invasion of England by Harald Hardrada ended in defeat and death for the Norwegian king, perhaps because of overconfidence after initial success against local forces, but also due to a strong surprise attack by English forces.

In 1171 the city of Dublin was captured by Richard de Clare the 2nd Earl of Pembroke and his Hiberno-Norman forces causing many of the city's Norse inhabitants to leave the old city.

In 1262 troops loyal to Scottish king Alexander III repelled the forces of King Hákon IV of Norway at the Battle of Largs. The battle was inconclusive, but Hákon died soon afterwards while wintering in Orkney, leaving matters to be settled by peace treaties rather than the battlefield.

The Vikings were forced to adopt and adapt to the changing world around them. They settled in new lands, learned new languages, adopted new cultures, established far reaching trading routes, intermarried, and blended with the population wherever they went.

The descendants of the Vikings, the Normans had also conquered and controlled territories as far away as the Holy Land during the Crusades. The Anglo-French War of 1202-1214 divided and diminished the Norman influence on England, as English Normans became English, and French Normans became French, and Norman civilisation as a cultural whole disappeared.

Sources

Anglo-Saxon Chronicle (B, The Abingdon Chronicle I), 787 (789): Cotton MS Tiberius A VI, ff 1r–35v
2021, Unknown, 10th century, British Library, London, 2012,
http://www.bl.uk/manuscripts/Viewer.aspx?ref=cotton_ms_tiberius_a_vi_f013r

Anglo-Saxon Chronicle (D, The Worcester Chronicle), 793: Cotton MS Tiberius B IV, ff. 3r- 86v 2021,
Unknown, 11th century, British Library, London, 2012,
http://www.bl.uk/manuscripts/Viewer.aspx?ref=cotton_ms_tiberius_b_iv_f026v

Anglo-Saxon Chronicle (D, The Worcester Chronicle), 948: Cotton MS Tiberius B IV, ff. 3r- 86v 2021,
Unknown, 11th century, British Library, London, 2012,
https://www.bl.uk/manuscripts/Viewer.aspx?ref=cotton_ms_tiberius_b_iv_f051r

Anglo-Saxon Chronicle (E, The Peterborough Chronicle), 952 & 964: Laud misc. 636, Unknown, 12th
century, Bodleian Library, Oxford, 2018, https://digital.bodleian.ox.ac.uk/objects/6272311c-058d-417a-
8e21-05e463b4f1f9/surfaces/9dc138d3-ba0d-4bc8-a7ca-4af976487187/

Anglo-Saxon Chronicle (E, The Peterborough Chronicle), 952 & 964: Laud misc. 636, Unknown, 12th
century, Bodleian Library, Oxford, 2018, https://digital.bodleian.ox.ac.uk/objects/6272311c-058d-417a-
8e21-05e463b4f1f9/surfaces/4febf20b-483c-4222-be11-3ce439f72a99/

Anglo-Saxon Chronicle (F, The Bilingual Canterbury Epitome), 870: Cotton MS Domitian A VIII, ff 30r-
70v 2021, Unknown, 11th century, British Library, London, 2012,
http://www.bl.uk/manuscripts/Viewer.aspx?ref=cotton_ms_tiberius_a_vi_f018r

Annales Bertiniani (Annals of Saint Bertin), 850: MGH SS 1, Waitz, Georg (Ed.), 1826, Die digitalen
Monumenta Germaniae Historica (dMGH), Hannover & Leipzig, 2004,
https://www.dmgh.de/mgh_ss_1/index.htm#page/445/mode/1up

Annales Bertiniani (Annals of Saint Bertin), 858: MGH SS 1, Waitz, Georg (Ed.), 1826, Die digitalen
Monumenta Germaniae Historica (dMGH), Hannover & Leipzig, 2004,
https://www.dmgh.de/mgh_ss_1/index.htm#page/451/mode/1up

Annales Fontanellenses (Annals of Fontanelle), 855, Pertz, Georg Heinrich (Ed.), 1829, Die digitalen
Monumenta Germaniae Historica (dMGH), Hannover & Leipzig, 2004,
https://web.archive.org/web/20181203055459/https://www.dmgh.de/de/fs1/object/display/bsb0000086
9_00325.html

Annales Xantenses (Annals of Xanten), 845: MGH SS rer. Germ. 12, Pertz, Georg Heinrich (Ed.),
1888, Die digitalen Monumenta Germaniae Historica (dMGH), Hannover & Leipzig, 2004,
https://www.dmgh.de/mgh_ss_rer_germ_12/index.htm#page/14/mode/1up

Annales Xantenses (Annals of Xanten), 873: MGH SS rer. Germ. 12, Pertz, Georg Heinrich (Ed.),
1888, Die digitalen Monumenta Germaniae Historica (dMGH), Hannover & Leipzig, 2004,
https://www.dmgh.de/mgh_ss_rer_germ_12/index.htm#page/32/mode/1up

Annals of Ulster: MS. Rawl. B. 489, Unknown, 16th century, Bodleian Library, Ireland, 2019,
https://digital.bodleian.ox.ac.uk/objects/a5918f5a-2149-47bb-857e-0792bab8085a/surfaces/f0da7984-
11aa-419f-ab5d-16efb5c0622b/

Einhards Jahrbücher, 814, Einhard, Dr Abel Otto (Trans.), 1888, Die digitalen Monumenta Germaniae Historica (dMGH), Hannover & Leipzig, 2004, https://www.mgh-bibliothek.de/dokumente/b/b025198.pdf

Eiríks Saga Rauða (The Saga of Erik the Red): Norse Text, Translation, and Word List, Embleton, M. L. (Translator), 2021, Independent, London, 2021, 979-8467805504

Gesta Danorum: Saxonis Grammatici Danorum Historiae Libri XVI, Saxo Grammaticus, 1534, Universitätsbibliothek Basel, Switzerland, 2010, https://www.e-rara.ch/bau_1/content/zoom/889580

Gesta Hammaburgensis Ecclesiae Pontificum (Deeds of the Bishops of Hamburg): MGH SS rer. Germ. 2, Adam of Bremen, Schmeidler, B. (Editor), 3rd Ed., 1917, Die digitalen Monumenta Germaniae Historica (dMGH), Hannover & Leipzig, 2004, https://www.dmgh.de/mgh_ss_rer_germ_2/index.htm#page/38/mode/1up

Gesta Normannorum Ducum (Deeds of the Dukes of Normandy), 1060: pub. pour la première fois en français par M. Guizot, et suivie de la Vie de Guillaume-le-conquérant, par Guillaume de Poitiers, Guillaume de Jumiège, 1826, Hathitrust Digital Library, Paris, 2019, https://babel.hathitrust.org/cgi/pt?id=mdp.39015013753564&view=1up&seq=23&skin=2021

Grœnlendinga Saga (The Saga of the Greenlanders): Norse Text, Translation, and Word List, Embleton, M. L. (Translator), 13th century, Independent, London, 2021, 979-8464540590

Heimskringla: Haralds Saga Hárfagra, Snorri Sturluson, c1220s, Heimskringla.no, Iceland, 2020, https://heimskringla.no/wiki/Haraldz_saga_ins_hárfagra_(FJ)

Heimskringla: The Saga of Harald Fairhair (Haralds Saga Hárfagra), Snorri Sturluson, c1220s, Heimskringla.no, Iceland, 2020, https://heimskringla.no/wiki/Haraldz_saga_ins_h%C3%A1rfagra_(FJ)

Hervarar Saga ok Heiðreks (The Saga of Hervör and Heidrek), Unknown, 13th century, Netútgáfan (Online Version), Iceland, 1998, https://www.snerpa.is/net/index.html

Historia Anglorum (The History of the English), Henry of Huntingdon, Thomas Arnold M.A. (Editor), 1154, Longman & Co., London, 1879, 2009, https://archive.org/details/henriciarchidia00unkngoog/page/n265/mode/2up

Íslendingabók, Ari Þorgilsson, 12th century, Heimskringla.no, Iceland, 2013, http://www.heimskringla.no/wiki/%C3%8Dslendingab%C3%B3k

Knýtlinga Saga (The Saga of Cnut's Descendants), Óláfr Þórðarson, c1250s, Heimskringla.no, Iceland, 2020, http://www.heimskringla.no/wiki/Knytlinga_saga

Krákumál (The Lay of Kraka): The Sagas of Ragnar Lothbrok: Norse Text, Translation, and Word List, 2nd Ed., Embleton, M. L. (Translator), 2021, Independent, London, 2021, 979-8475152591

Landnámabók: Sturlubók, Sturla Þórðarson (Ed.) & Eiríkur Rögnvaldsson (Ed.), 13th century, Netútgáfan (Online Version), Iceland, 1998, https://www.snerpa.is/net/snorri/landnama.htm

Lausavísur (3) 'Þat mælti mín móðir': Chapter 40, Egill's Saga, Egill Skallagrimsson (poem), Snorri Sturluson (saga), 13th century, Netútgáfan (Online Version), Iceland, 1998, https://www.snerpa.is/net/isl/egils.htm

Letter from Alcuin to King Æthelred of Northumbria, c793, The Letter Book of Archbishop Wulfstan: Cotton MS Vespasian A XIV, ff 114–179 2021, Alcuin of York, 11th & 12th centuries, British Library, London, 2012, http://www.bl.uk/manuscripts/Viewer.aspx?ref=cotton_ms_vespasian_a_xiv_f126r>

Orkneyinga Saga: History of the Earls of Orkney, Orkneyinga Saga, 13th century, Heimskringla.no, Iceland, 2019, https://heimskringla.no/wiki/Orkneyinga_saga

Ragnars Saga Loðbrókar (The Saga of Ragnar Lothbrok): The Sagas of Ragnar Lothbrok: Norse Text, Translation, and Word List, 2nd Ed., Embleton, M. L. (Translator), 2021, Independent, London, 2021, 979-8475152591

Ragnarssona Þáttr (The Tale of Ragnar's Sons): The Sagas of Ragnar Lothbrok: Norse Text, Translation, and Word List, 2nd Ed., Embleton, M. L. (Translator), 2021, Independent, London, 2021, 979-8475152591

The Russian Primary Chronicles (Povest' Vremennykh Let, Повѣсть времмньныхъ лѣтъ): Laurentian Codex, F.p.IV.2, Unknown, 1377, National Library of Russia, St. Petersburg, 2012, http://expositions.nlr.ru/LaurentianCodex/_Project/page_Show.php?lang=en

Vita Ælfredi regis Angul Saxonum (The Life of Alfred King of the Anglo-Saxons), 893: Together with the Annals of St Neots erroneously ascribed to Asser, Asser, Stevenson, W. H. (Ed.), 1904, Clarendon Press, Oxford, 2014, https://archive.org/details/gri_33125000734208/page/138/mode/2up